Warrior

Book 7 of The Dangerous Series
Christian Romantic Suspense
A stand-alone novel

By Linda K. Rodante

Linda K. Rodante

The LORD is a warrior;
the LORD is his name.

Exodus 15:3 NIV

Scripture quotations marked KJV are from the King James Bible, Public Domain.

Scripture quotations marked NIV are taken from the Holy Bible, New International Version®, NIV®. Copyright © 1973, 1978, 1984, 2011 by Biblica, Inc.™ Used by permission of Zondervan. All rights reserved worldwide. www.zondervan.com The "NIV" and "New International Version" are trademarks registered in the United States Patent and Trademark Office by Biblica, Inc.™

Scripture quotations marked NKJV are taken from the New King James Version®. Copyright © 1982 by Thomas Nelson. Used by permission. All rights reserved.

Warrior

1.   a person engaged or experienced in warfare; a soldier.
2.   a person who shows or has shown great vigor, courage, or aggressiveness
https://www.dictionary.com/browse/warrior

Dedication

To my niece, Tiffany Knadle Ried, who at this moment is
fighting her own battle.
You are a warrior.
And
To the greatest truth-teller of all times: Jesus Christ.
You have enlightened our paths with your Word.

Chapter 1

For the weapons of our warfare are not carnal, but mighty
through God to the pulling down of strong holds.
(2 Corinthians 10:4 KJV)

Kati Walsh drove a gloved fist toward her opponent's face,
but Terry Johnson shot an arm up, blocked her punch,
and danced backward, grinning.

"Come on, girl. You're slow today."

Kati scowled. Sweat rolled down her back. Her pixie-cut
blonde hair clung to her face, but she bobbed forward, arms
up—protecting, waiting.

Terry jutted his chin and egged her on. "Come on. Come
on. Lay into me."

"You're gonna get...too cocky...one day." Kati's breath
huffed out between words.

"But not today." Terry threw a right jab that she barely
countered. His leg sliced a roundhouse kick into her side.

"*Oufff!*" She doubled over. The body armor they wore
wasn't much good against power punches or kicks, and as her
trainer and sparring partner, Terry knew it.

He laughed. "You should have known that was coming."

The spurt of anger squirted adrenaline throughout her body.
She'd take the adrenaline but keep her cool. She concentrated
on the next combination. Left foot jab, jab, straight right, left
hook kick. Terry parried and blocked each one with ease. He

came back with a jab, straight right, left hook, and a right spinning back kick. She was familiar with his moves and managed to block or step away from the combination, but the spinning back kick almost caught her. He laughed again as she stumbled and righted herself.

Her breath hitched, but the adrenaline rush gave her one more jolt of energy. She made a small weight shift and threw an uppercut. Her glove smashed into his jaw. He flew back, slammed against the ropes, and dropped to his knees.

She wove back and forth, gloves up, and stared down at him. "You should have known that was coming, Terry."

Too bad the spiritual demons she battled these days didn't fall as easy.

***

Reece Jernigan stood in the shadows outside the boxing ring. The Florida sun forced the building's air conditioners to work overtime, and he was glad for his cutoff jeans and the short-sleeved polo. A T-shirt would have been nice, but not in this neighborhood...

He glanced to his right, wondering why Josh insisted on khaki Dockers and a white long-sleeved shirt each day. Josh didn't have Reece's tattoos to hide, so his need for the "uniform" made no sense. At least today Josh had rolled up his sleeves and left the tie in the SUV.

A loud grunt came from the boxing ring. The woman bounced on her feet but kept her eyes on the man on the platform. He had one glove on the ropes and struggled to stand.

Reece turned to Joshua and lifted his brows.

Josh returned the look and grinned. "Well, don't make her mad, bro. Remember the pastor's wife said she might not be happy we're here to pick her up." He lifted his chin, indicating the woman in the ring. "And don't pull any of your stunts, expecting me to save your hide."

Reece snorted. "No worry there. You always leave me hanging."

"You give me no credit for extricating you from the traps you set for yourself."

"Extricating? What's *extricating* mean? No one understands what you say, Josh. How does that help me?" He turned his attention back to the sparring mat.

The woman leaned over and said something to the man. He grimaced, mouthed something, and stood to his feet. She bit her lip, an obvious attempt to hide a smile.

Reece chuckled. "Come on. Let's go get the Battle Maiden before she does another number on her sparring partner. He looks like he's asking for it."

"See? That's what I mean. Battle Maiden. You've got a name for everyone, and not everyone's enamored with them."

Reece muttered "enamored" under his breath and walked past Joshua toward the ring.

The woman's breath huffed from her chest, but her bouncing slowed. The spiky blonde hair was matted with sweat. "I apologize, Terr. I didn't mean to hit you that hard."

The other boxer rubbed his jaw, face contorted. "It's not a competition, Kati. You ought to be careful, or you might find yourself on the ropes next time—or with your face messed up."

The man straightened and threw a feinted punch. She rocked back and blocked, her eyes widening.

Terry laughed. "Gotcha, babe."

The girl frowned. "I told you not to call me babe."

Reece stepped closer. "That *gotcha* would work better if she hadn't already sent you to the mat with a real punch."

"Reece." Josh's voice cautioned.

The man glared. "Who are you?"

Reece nodded at Kati. "Came to give a ride to the winner. Looks like that would be the lady."

The woman's focus moved his way. Her green eyes studied him. "You did, did you? Then I'll have to repeat Terry's question. Who are you?"

Joshua put a hand on Reece's arm and moved up beside him. "I'm Josh Corbin. The new assistant pastor at New Life Church. Pastor Alan sent me to pick you up. He said your car was being worked on, that his wife—Daneen?—was supposed to give you a ride home, but they have an unexpected meeting. He also said you wouldn't have your phone on you, so you probably wouldn't know."

Reece grinned. No lie. Not in that outfit. The girl's eyes narrowed when she caught his stare, and Joshua's head swiveled around. Reece sobered.

"Ask him for an ID, Kati." Terry bobbed forward. "They both look suspicious to me."

Joshua dug for his wallet, flipped it open, and shoved it in her direction. "Pastor Alan did send a text to your phone. You can go get your phone and read it."

She glanced at his ID. "I don't really need this. I know your name. Knew you were coming to the church today." Her gaze slid to Reece. "And you are?"

"This is Reece Jernigan. He's the friend who brought me. He's also looking for a job…" Josh glanced around the gym, looked at them inquiringly.

Reece sent him a scowl. "Thanks for the help, *friend*, but I'm fine on that score."

Joshua's mouth hitched, and he turned back to the woman. "We can wait until you're finished." He nodded at the man, Terry, and walked back into the shadowed corner where they'd stood before.

Reece glanced around the gym before following. Yeah, he and a gym like this? Not again. Not in a million years. "What was that about, dude?"

"Just giving you something to think about besides the Battle Maiden."

Reece's look skipped back to the rink. He eyed the girl as she raised her gloves. A kickboxer. With a rock-solid uppercut.

Nice.

A motor revved outside, followed by a screech of wheels. The sound circled the building, halted. A minute later, someone gunned the engine. Once. Twice. Three times. Then circled the building again.

Reece concentrated on the sound. Motorcycle. Something niggled inside him. He frowned, listened to the sound again, and then moved past Joshua toward the front door.

"Hold the fort, man."

As he neared the door, the unmistakable smell of gasoline hit him. He picked up his pace. Premonition hit every nerve. He slid in front of the doorway. On the other side of the glass, fire leapt from a burning container to the ground. The bushes and walkway in front of the door appeared wet with accelerant. An engine roared, and a motorcycle disappeared around the building's corner. Reece stared. Flames jumped skyward and raced for the building.

He turned and ran. "Fire! Fire out front! Where's the back entrance? Fire!" He sprinted toward the ring.

Josh ran up beside him. "What's going on?"

"Someone set a fire out front. Grab the girl and her partner." He hollered at the other boxers and members. "Fire! Fire out front! Where's the back door?"

Someone pointed. He threw his hand in that direction, pointing toward the back, and took off at a run. A huge whoosh came from the front doors. Someone screamed. Others hollered and ran toward the back. Those working out looked his way. He dashed across the gym. "Fire at the front doors! Get out!"

Everyone began running. Those from the changing areas appeared, pulling on clothes, alarm on their faces.

A man and a woman neared the back door.

"Don't go out that door!" Reece roared. "Stop!" His three years out of the trenches could cost them. "Don't go out that door!"

The woman skidded to a halt, and Reece grabbed the shirt

collar of the man in front of him. "Let me make sure it's safe."

The girl stepped aside, eyes wide. "Go ahead."

"Out of the way!" yelled someone else.

Reece stepped in their path and put up a hand. "Wait here. All of you, wait here."

He looked past them, found Josh's tall figure along with the sparring couple. "Keep them back. I need to check outside." He slipped the Glock from the holster at his back and stopped by the door.

Motorcycle. Gasoline. An intentional fire.

It didn't leave him with a good feeling.

He stilled the noise in his head, stepped to the door, twisted the knob, and thrust it open. Nothing. He waited a moment, trying to hear over the clamor of voices behind him. Gun up, he slid his head past the door, then jerked backward.

A man straddled a motorcycle outside. One person. Brown skinned, tattoos, biker jacket, and smirk. Behind him, in the empty parking lot, the streetlight had clicked on, leaving an eerie glow.

Reece shot another look at Josh, the girl Kati, and her sparring partner. They stood in front of the others, but their eyes were on him. Terry's gaze darted to the front door and back. A wall of flames mixed with the rising smoke on the other side of the gym. Reece waved them back against the wall. Most moved, but Terry yelled at him. Reece held up the gun, sent a narrow-eyed stare, and everyone quieted.

He turned to the door again, eased his head forward. The man on the motorcycle revved its engine. His mouth showed a wide, uneven sneer before he laughed and screeched down the street.

Reece's gaze flicked right and left. Nothing, no one else. He holstered his gun and waved the others forward. They scrambled and pushed past him, but he caught Terry's arm.

"Who's in charge here? Is everyone out?"

The other man snatched his arm free. "I am. I'm in charge.

It's my gym." His face had whitened. "It's on fire! Everything I've poured into it. My life!"

Reece nodded. Emotion ricocheted through him, but he moved his gaze back to the street. "Are you sure everyone's out?"

Terry's sparring partner, Kati, leaned forward. "Unless someone slipped in after you, everybody is here." She turned toward Terry, her hand resting on his arm. "I'm sorry, Terr. So sorry."

The shock on his face echoed the look in his eyes. "I can't believe he actually did it."

"He? Who are you talking about?"

Josh caught Reece's gaze. "I called 911."

"Good." Reece examined those milling around, taking in their reactions. His focus shifted to Terry. "He? There was a biker out here."

Terry's mouth opened. He swallowed. "What did he look like?"

"Hispanic maybe, but tall. Young. A gang member?"

Sirens sounded in the distance. Terry's eyes half closed. "He wanted insurance money." When he twisted back to the building, his face seemed to dissolve. "Or he said this would happen."

"This was a warning. He left you and the others alive, in one piece. Next time they might be outside waiting for you."

The girl gasped. Reece's eyes shifted her way.

The color disappeared from her face, leaving green eyes to search his. "Who are you anyway? A cop or something?"

Red and blue lights and pulsating sirens rounded the corner. Police cruisers appeared. A red fire engine rocked to its side, rounding the building. Men and women poured from the vehicles.

Reece watched the quick, decisive movements of the firefighters. "No. No one in particular. No one important."

***

Kati shifted the large box in her arms and kicked a knock-knock on the door. At least her kickboxing came in good for something—so far sharing about her faith at the gym had not. Her heart squeezed. What would Terry do now? What would the members do? She'd call soon, but she didn't want to inundate him when she knew others would be calling. She would pray and leave the solution in God's hands.

"Come in!" The voice sounded strange and stressed, but she recognized it from the aftermath of the fire and the drive home two days ago.

She tapped again with her foot, and a moment later the door flew open. Joshua stood looking at her, brows high, his face echoing the tone of his voice.

"Sorry, but my hands were full." She indicated the box with her chin.

He eyed it for a second, then reached and hoisted it out of her arms. When he stepped away from the door, he waved her into the room.

"Come in. Come in. Have you got your car back then?" His gaze went from the box and back to her. "What's all this?"

"Yes, to the car. Thanks for asking. And this is just some office equipment that was buried in a back closet here. I thought you might need it. We haven't had an assistant pastor in years, and this office hasn't been used forever, so…"

He nodded and looked around the room. Papers and books littered the desk. Other boxes and books filled the two chairs and lined the walls.

"Although maybe you won't need…"

Josh made a sweep with his arm. "Does this look like chaos to you?"

"Can I take the fifth?"

He grinned, the stress lines easing. "Setting up home and an office and preparing for my first sermon here—well, this equals my first jump from an airplane."

"A bit unusual." Kati nodded. The congregation had talked about the new assistant pastor over the last month, but their nervousness, she realized, did not match his. "We watched the videos of your preaching and FaceTimed. We're good. Relax, Pastor."

He shot her a grateful smile, moved books from a chair, and waved her into it. "Wired into the whole congregation for a one-on-three-hundred conversation also ranked up there."

His smile was engaging, and so was the loose limbered way he moved. Like a cheetah, she decided. Long, lean, and wiry. She laughed at his expression. "That *was* interesting."

He pulled open the box and dug through it. "Looks like good stuff. How'd you know I needed this?"

"That was pretty easy when I thought about Pastor Alan and Daneen having to go out of town."

Joshua stopped, looked over the box at her. "Such a shock for him, his brother dying like that. No warning."

Kati nodded. Sadness washed through her. "He is such a great guy. He and Daneen both are wonderful. He would be here for you if he could."

"I know. I'm not worried about that." His mouth inched up on one side. "Just a little flustered trying to get settled in."

Kati glanced around the office and identified the smell that wrinkled her nose. "You've already painted."

"Here and at the house. Reece is handy with most stuff, and he keeps me going. I'd sit and spend the time on the sermon if he'd let me."

"Ah. The slave driver. Martha to your Mary? I might have guessed that." She hesitated. During the ride back to her place two days ago, the two men's conversation had proved amusing and interesting. "Is Reece your brother?"

Joshua pulled plastic desk organizers, a stapler, tape, pens, a desk caddie, and other items from the box she'd brought. "Martha to my Mary, huh? I'll have to tell him that." The small

15

grin showed his amusement. Then he put his head back, and his look changed. "A blood brother? No. But a friend that sticks closer than a brother? Yes."

Hmmm… Kati leaned back in the chair. Their looks were completely different—Josh tall and blond with blue eyes, Reece stockier, dark hair and eyes—so she hadn't expected them to be related, but you never knew. "That's something to say about someone."

"Yes, it is. What about you, Kati? Who are your close friends at church? Are your parents here? Siblings?"

"Friends? Let's see. Lynn Richards. You'll meet her and her husband, Detective Rich Richards. He's been pushing for a security team at the church." Kati hesitated. "And Ryann Byrd's a close friend. Although she doesn't attend much anymore. And you'll need to know Miss Eleanor, our eighty-eight-year-old prayer warrior."

"Ah. I'll need to get with Rich Richards. And you said a prayer warrior? I'll definitely invite her and anyone else that does combat in that arena to lunch soon." He sat back on the edge of the desk and crossed his arms.

His grin warmed her.

"I want to establish a regular prayer meeting to pray for the neighborhood and for unsaved friends and relatives."

"I'd love that, and we have a group who will love it, too."

His blue eyes focused on her. Wow. Could those eyes see through her? Feeling suddenly nervous, she stood.

"I'd better let you finish your work." When she started for the door, she realized that he'd left it open. Good move.

"Kati." He came off the desk then stopped. The smile reappeared. "Thank you for bringing these." He waved his hand to the things on his desk.

"You're welcome. And welcome to New Life Church."

He nodded. "Thank you again. But what about your family? Are they here, too?"

"My…family?" She tried not to stutter.

"Yes."

A movement at the doorway caused her to turn. Reece stepped into the room. His brown eyes caught hers, and a light appeared in them. He held a bag from a local deli and two bottles of water. The scent of garlic and warm bread floated her way.

"Hello, Reece." Her voice gushed. She couldn't stop it. "I see you brought lunch. That's good. I'll just go and let you two eat. Good talking to you, Pastor." She scooted by Reece and out the door. She could feel his eyes on her as she hurried down the hallway.

"What did you do to the lady, Josh?" Reece's voice followed her. "Or was it just me?"

Chapter 2

Also he went down and slew a lion in a pit on a snowy day.
(1Chronicles 11:22 KJV)

The kitten seemed frozen on the branch above her head.

"You've been out here hollering all during class, little one. Why won't you come to me?" Her Sunday Bible class for teen girls had been interrupted by numerous pleas from the girls to rescue the "poor baby." She'd finally agreed to have one of the boys save it after class. And she'd searched for someone to help but couldn't find one of the older teens, so she'd come herself.

Perhaps not a smart idea…

She inched forward along the tree limb. The slight give left her with an uneasy feeling. Where were the girls? You'd think a few would come out to support her in rescuing the "baby." Oh well, she'd do almost anything to keep the girls coming to the class. In this day and age, she knew the blessing of having twenty girls in attendance.

She reached toward the kitten. "Come on, baby. Come on."

She should have found Jake. He would have done it. After all, he rescued people from the Gulf of Mexico, from the waters off Clearwater Beach, all the time. He could certainly get a kitten down from a tree. Right?

"I'm here to help you, little one. Come on." She kicked off the cute, smooth-bottomed shoes she'd worn for church. Barefoot would be much better. As her tender skin settled on the oak's rough bark, she grimaced. Maybe not on that score either. She searched for another hold, closer to the feline, easing both feet along the limb.

The cat leapt for her head, and Kati screamed. A flurry of paws and claws raked her hair. She screamed again and threw up a hand to protect her eyes. The kitten scrambled over her, across the branch, and down the tree.

Her feet slithered sideways, and her one-handed hold slipped. She flung the free arm back toward the overhead branch, clawing at it. Her hand missed, slipped. She teetered and made a frantic eye search for another handhold. At the same time, she shoved backward against the trunk, her mind grasping at how to save herself.

Her foot slid off the oak's limb, and she fell forward. As she grabbed for another hold, her body dropped like a barbell from a high wall and yanked both arms from their sockets. Or so it felt. She dangled from the tree. Her own weight and the pain jarred through her.

"Hold on!"

The shouted words weren't much encouragement, because she knew she couldn't. Seconds later, the coarse bark scraped free of her fingers and palms, and she dropped—only to be sacked like a quarterback before she hit the ground. She crumbled forward, and the linebacker's body rolled over hers.

She groaned and shoved at the shoulder in her chest. Reece rolled backward, a grimace on his face.

"Ohhhh..." She clamped her mouth shut before she said anything else. It would not be Christian or ladylike. Some of that other life still surfaced.

Reece grunted and pushed himself up. "Wow. Are you okay?"

"Not sure." The man had just slammed her like a mixed martial arts fighter doing a takedown. How should she be?

His look showed concern, and then, as he saw her expression, the dark eyes lit with amusement. "The next time you

LINDA K. RODANTE

climb a tree, please tell me first. That way I won't have to save you at a dead run."

"Save me?" Her voice skidded into high. "More like crush my ribs."

Next to them, the ground pounded and other feet skidded to a halt. Kati forced her head around.

Joshua stood over them, dark eyes wide, alarmed. "Kati, are you okay? What happened?" His look jumped from her to Reece and back.

Other people gathered around. Heat climbed up her throat. She took Joshua's outstretched hand, stood, and brushed off the dress pants she wore.

"Don't worry about me, bro." Reece stood, too. "I just tried to save the girl."

"I saw."

Joshua's expression made Kati choke on a laugh.

"Kati!"

The female voice wrenched her head around. Ryann Byrd pushed past the small crowd that had gathered.

"Ryann, you're here." Kati couldn't keep the warmth and surprise from her voice. As the young woman embraced her, Kati hugged back.

Her friend freed herself. "What happened?"

Others chimed in, and the heat surged back into Kati's face. Her gaze darted around the group. Reece stood back, arms across his chest, eyes lit but face with the same inquisitive expression as everyone else.

Joshua tilted his head. "When I saw feet dangling from the tree, I thought it was one of the youth."

Okay, heat was not the word. Her face probably looked like glowing coals after a tailgate party. She bit her lip, took a deep breath, and blurted, "A kitten."

"A kitten?" Complete bafflement on Joshua's face, but Reece straightened. One side of his mouth rose, as if guessing what her next words would be.

20

"She was saving the kitten." Becky, one of the girls from her Bible class, spoke up.

"Yeah," another one said. "She promised us. She said she would save it."

"No, she said she'd get someone to save it."

Ryann gaped at her. "You were saving a kitten?" She sent a look up the tree. Others did the same.

Someone laughed, followed by more laughter.

Joshua leaned forward. "Did you get him? Or her?"

"She jumped past me just when I thought I had her."

"And made it down herself?" Reece's amusement sounded in his voice. He shook his head and turned with the others heading back to the church.

Giggling and laughter floated back to her.

Ryann stared at her. "You are crazy, you know that?"

"I know." She shrugged. "Ryann, this is Joshua Corbin, our new assistant pastor."

Ryann shoved long hair from her face. "Hello."

Joshua held out his hand. "Hello, Ryann. I'm glad I got to meet you. A friend of Kati's is a friend of mine."

"Oh, yeah. Thanks."

Kati nudged her. "Let's head back. We might miss the new pastor's sermon."

Joshua fell in step beside them. "Yeah, and I'm not sure how, but I bet he'll work in something about saving lions from trees." His voice changed. "Or maybe being saved from lions."

"Lions?"

"Well, it sounds better than *kitten*, doesn't it?"

"If you can work that in, I'll buy you dinner."

He laughed. "You'll have to stand in line. I think I have every Sunday dinner scheduled for the next six weeks."

"That would be our church. Sunday dinners are a big thing. And if you need work done on a Saturday, we have a group that does lunches then, too."

***

His usual morning routine of rising early, prayer, Bible study, and seeking God had given him nothing.

Of course he trusted God. Joshua had told himself that at least five times over the last hour, and each time he'd thrown a look upward, as if to ask the Creator of the universe if he knew what time it was. His first sermon at his first church had loomed in less than twenty minutes when he'd heard the scream. His view through the office window had shown the same thing Reece must have seen. A pair of legs dangling from a tree. He'd made it to the door, through the hall, and out into the field in record time.

Of course, Reece had made it faster. Go figure.

He smiled now and eyed the podium. His concentration pinged from God to the worship leader to the congregation. God was faithful. He'd dropped the message into Josh's heart as soon as Joshua said the word "lion."

The message exploded inside, whole, together. Not long, but to the point. And he prayed as he'd prayed earlier that their hearts would be open, that they'd be like Ezekiel's dry bones—ready to rise, ready for the Holy Spirit's breath.

He had no doubt that trouble brewed somewhere. Reece stood near the back, his impassive features telling Josh more about his friend's tension than anything else. Saving Kati from the fall this morning had probably been good for him. But the trouble Josh worried about would not come from Reece. No, it would come from the Enemy, and that vagabond would most likely use a stalwart member of the church, someone everyone respected, someone who hated change.

He closed his eyes, sighed. A person he himself would re-spect and love. But time enough for that later. The last stanza of the final song ended. His eyes rose once more, looking to the author and finisher of his faith. He stepped forward.

"Lord, we welcome you. Holy Spirit, we welcome you. Je-

22

sus, we welcome you. Thank you for your presence." He lifted his head and smiled. "We serve a wonderful God, don't we?"

Murmurs of agreement moved throughout the sanctuary.

Thank you, Lord, that they're responsive. Grab their hearts. Grab them.

"I appreciate the worship and the fact that this group, this worship leader, wants to reach God and not just entertain. Thank you."

He searched for the man, Emmanuel Rodriguez—Manny, he was called—whom he'd only met a day ago, and he let his gaze settle on him. He and the other music members had slipped off the stage the moment Joshua began to speak.

"I also want to thank everyone for their support and for your welcome. FaceTime and YouTube are not like meeting people in person. And I finally was able to meet a number of you in person this week." His grin touched Kati and others, slipping over the congregation, before it stopped on Reece.

Reece nodded at him, the impassive look gone. Instead something in the eyes and the line of his mouth said to Joshua, "Get with it."

Joshua inhaled and straightened to his full six-foot-one height. "A lady fell from a tree today." The rustle of laughter rose. Many looked Kati's way. News spread fast, as always. "She'd climbed up to rescue a kitten. I'm here to tell you that God is looking for rescuers today. He's looking for those that will stand in the lion's den like Daniel, knowing that the lions have no power over them. Who will chase a lion into a pit on a snowy day like Benaiah did. Or, like Samson, tear apart a lion with his bare hands. He is looking for warriors today, for an army."

Someone shifted in the pews; another person cleared their throat. Eyes fastened on him.

"I'm calling out dry bones today. You've been sitting in these pews long enough. You know there's more. You've asked and prayed for more. God has heard your cry. I call out to the dry bones today. Come alive. God wants an army. Come alive!"

***

The sermon, of course, had generated texts and emails and phone calls. Kati rested against the seat of Reece's black Range Rover Sport. Older model but well maintained. The last few days had exhausted her. Between work and the constant comments on the sermon—for, against, and in between—she looked forward to some time away from it.

Reece's head turned. "Thanks for coming. I'm sure Mrs. Willis will feel better seeing you than just some guy she doesn't know. Especially me. Sometimes I get a nervous stare when I show up at someone's place."

"You? Nah. I can't see that. The mega tats and hard-eyed, get-in-line attitude. Why would you make anyone nervous?"

A look from the corner of his eyes slid her way. "*Mega* tats? You haven't been to New York."

"I notice you didn't argue with the other description."

His mouth curled. "Comes in handy sometimes. And you, Miss Always Available for Ministry, showed at the right time today."

Kati sent him a rueful look before she smiled. The after-church get-together Joshua had spontaneously planned this past Sunday had given her more information on the assistant pastor and Reece. Joshua had talked with and entertained everyone with descriptions of moving to Florida, their times at the beach, and the first sunburns of the newly initiated. Reece, on the other hand, had held back, unsmiling, watching the crowd as if he were part of the Secret Service that guarded the president, until Joshua made jokes at Reece's expense. After the third one, Reece had added one of his own, and the back-and-forth after that had the whole group laughing.

Now they were on their way to Reece's place—or rather

the house in which he and Joshua were living, picking up food that Joshua had purchased to take to Mrs. Willis' house. Homes always provided good information about people and their lives. She'd have to see what this revealed.

Reece returned her smile, and he brought the SUV to a stop in front of an older home. Kati glanced up and down the street. An older, run-down neighborhood. She couldn't help the glance of surprise she sent him. Not what she'd envisioned.

The corners of his eyes crinkled. "Joshua's idea is if we want to get to know the people we're ministering to, then we should live where they do. Not unlike my own neighborhood in New York. We've done some work on the place though."

They climbed out and headed to the front door.

"When did you have the time?"

"Between midnight and four in morning." His mouth lifted. "And I'm sorry to leave you out here, but Josh has strict rules. Can't have beautiful women in the house unless accompanied by an eighty-year-old grandmother. A pastor' life—or assistant pastor's—is filled with dos and don'ts. And therefore mine is, too."

"No problem. It's a good rule. Besides, it's a beautiful day. I'll just hang out on the swing here if you don't mind."

"I'll be back in a minute." Reece disappeared into the house.

The swing seemed like a new addition, and Kati noticed the hummingbird feeder and flowers in the corners of the porch. Nice. *Surprised two bachelors would think of those.* The porch railing had been sanded and finished recently. She glanced behind her. Yep. A fresh coat of paint on the wall, too. The guys had worked hard. From the looks of the other houses lining the streets, no one else bothered much with the outside of their homes. No, she studied a house three doors down and one on the corner. Flowers clung close to the homes in both lawns. Some people did care.

Or could afford to, Kati corrected herself. Some owners on

this street wouldn't be able to afford much. She leaned her head back. The wind lifted her hair, stroked the back of her neck. An assistant pastor's salary wasn't much, though, and she had no idea what Reece did.

The door opened behind her, and Reece dropped down onto the swing. "Josh said he left that bag of groceries on the table, but it's not there. Let me text him."

She nodded and waited, content to watch the storm clouds rising past the roofs on the other side of the street. They had predicted rain…

Reece's phone rang. The banter between the two men showed their humor as well as their affection for each other. Nice.

Reece put the phone away a moment later. "He walked out to his car while we were talking, and guess what?"

"I heard. He put it in the car this morning and forgot?"

"He's becoming an old man at twenty-nine."

The breeze kicked up, and a plastic bag blew past the house. "Well, he's got a lot on him since Pastor Alan left for his brother's funeral."

"Yeah. From what Joshua said, they won't be back for a few weeks. Alan has to deal with his brother's estate since there's no one else. It will give the congregation a chance to get to know Josh." He turned. "Not everyone is like you, Ms. Walsh, pitching in to make the new pastor welcome, especially after Sunday's sermon."

Ah. So they would get to it.

She tilted her head and surveyed him. "Are you wondering where I stand?"

He shrugged. "You're back today. That's a good indicator."

"I liked it. Think we needed it—a call to get up and start working. Don't sit on our backsides in the pews."

The amusement showed again. "I guess you did like it."

"God calling us deeper. I told Joshua the other day that we have a prayer group that's been praying for this."

"And you help with the widows and orphans."

She shot him another glance. "We don't have any orphans."

"But if we did…"

"I'd help."

"I thought so. I'm a little surprised someone your age is doing that."

"And what age am I supposed to be?"

Wind stirred around them. Across from the way, behind the houses, the dark clouds gathered. Kati stared at them. Was he trying to say something?

"Just, well, usually these things are done by some grandmotherly type, aren't they?"

"What things?"

"Making the new pastor feel welcome, helping him set up his office, letting him know the needs of the church and the community."

Kati stared at the sky. Did she look desperate? Is that what he thought? When she only wanted to help? The charcoal clouds bunched together. The wind picked up. "I didn't mean to be underfoot. I just wanted Joshua to feel welcome. With Pastor Alan running off and Joshua not knowing anyone or having a chance to get his feet on the ground or anything, I thought he could use someone stepping up."

"It's nice what you've done. For Josh—and for Mrs. Willis."

"That was Josh. I just told him that she had no one and lived on Social Security, and he said the church was supposed to help widows."

"But you've been doing that, haven't you? That's why Joshua bought those groceries on the way home yesterday. You've been doing it, and he wanted to take the burden off you."

Kati winced. So, Joshua had passed on that information. She'd have to watch what she said. "Everybody needs help now and then."

"Yes, they do."

"Did I make it past your scrutiny?"

His mouth hitched. "You're an enigma, Ms. Walsh. I'm trying to figure you out. It's what I do. Nothing personal."

"Nothing to figure out."

"Then what do you do?"

"For a living, you mean?" She could ask him the same thing.

"Yeah. You seem to have free days…"

"Are you wondering if I'm independently wealthy?"

"That would be one answer."

"And the other is, I have a nice cushy job where I can take off whenever I want."

"Or the truth might be…"

"That I'm a nurse who works twelve-hour shifts and has half of the week to do what I want—whether sleep or help around the church."

"You're a nurse?"

"Why do I hear surprise?"

"I have no idea. I just…I love it. You can beat people up and fix them afterwards."

"Or I could just beat them up and leave them." She added sarcasm to her voice.

He laughed. "Okay. Sorry I overstepped. Look, we have to go back to the church to get that bag of groceries." Rain swirled onto the porch. He shoved the swing back. "Hey!"

Wind tossed a shower at them. They both jumped at the same time. Reece grabbed her hand and pulled her toward the door. He threw it open.

"Quick! Get in. Get in."

Kati scooted into the house, followed by daggers of rain. "What about the rules?"

"The rules are officially broken." He shoved the door closed. "Wow. Do storms always come that quickly?"

"Not usually."

"Hmm." He turned and caught her expression. "What?"

"Nothing."

"Uh-huh. I'm from New York, did I say? I'm still getting used to the southern laid-back way of living here and the weather. The Gulf, by the way, is incredible. Water as far as you can see. I'm used to streets and more streets and row houses. You run for any shelter when it rains."

"But you have snow up there."

"Yeah. I'm also inside when it snows."

Kati shook her head. "You're missing the best part. Walking in the snow." She glanced around the room. Typical male stuff. Dark leather couch. Large chairs and a wooden coffee table. On top of this sat books and coffee mugs, used, she'd bet. "But where's your accent?"

"My accent? As compared to yours, Miss Southern?"

"I'm from Florida. I don't have an accent."

"Who are you kidding? It's not Alabama, but it's southern."

She rested her hands on her hips. "But you don't have that New York accent I've heard from others."

"Because my mother was from Virginia, my dad from Ohio, my grandparents from Idaho. I heard all sorts of accents growing up." He turned to the windows. "Well, that's stopping. Fast shower. A gust of wind, and it's gone."

His phone rang, and he pulled it from the holster on his belt. "What's up, dude?" He sent Kati a comical face. "Head of the security team? No, I'd vote for that detective that's part of the congregation."

It had to be Joshua. Whoa. He was on top of things.

After a moment's pause, Reece growled into the phone. "No, bro. You heard me."

Kati waved toward the front door. She'd let them fight this out. She stepped onto the porch and made a beeline to the swing. Soaked. Umm… *So stand and admire the houses with the few flowers, girl.*

Her mind returned to Joshua's message on Sunday. He'd prophesied over them. He'd called them forth. The way he spoke made God so real. Of course, he was…but just like the others, she'd sat in the pews each week and went home to her safe life. Only she pretended she didn't. She helped around the church, helped those like Mrs. Willis, doing everything except reaching those who were lost. Not that both weren't needed, but when God put his finger on what you'd been avoiding…

She hugged herself. What had Joshua alluded to when he said later that they wouldn't be pew sitters for long?

A roar came from around the street corner, and three motorcycles appeared. Kati watched as they rode pass. Big bikes. One of the men sent her a grin. *Oops, Kati. Don't stare at men in the neighborhood.*

A half block down the bikers made a U-turn and headed back. Something jolted inside her. Uh-oh. Should she beat a hasty retreat to the door? But that would look cowardly. Besides, wasn't this what she was just thinking? These could be three nice neighbors of Reece's and Joshua's that she should get to know.

The motorcycles stopped in front of the house, and the man who'd leered at her climbed off, his dark eyes raking her. The back of her neck tightened. She forced her feet to stay put.

Where was Reece?

Her gaze darted away from the man's, but she caught the smirks of the other two and switched her focus back to him as he stepped onto the walkway.

His sleeveless leather vest showed muscled and tattooed arms. One large tattoo climbed the right side of his face. Long brown hair and brown skin accented intense black eyes.

This didn't feel good. She stepped toward the front steps and put up a hand. "Please wait. I'm not the owner of the house. You can come back later if you want to meet him."

The man slowed. "Sorry to hear that, but I wasn't interested in the man."

He started forward again, and Kati moved to the middle of the steps. "I asked you to wait." She squared herself off.

The man's grin widened. "You want to fight me, señorita?" He threw a look backward.

Laughter rose from the other two.

She realized she'd pulled her arms in, fists cuffed. Her mind threw up a prayer, and she forced herself to relax. "No, sorry, but I told you I don't live here."

"That's too bad, pequeña." He waved to the flowers. "Like these, you would add beauty to the neighborhood."

Snickers came from the road. His leer returned, and he advanced once more.

The door opened behind her. She turned her head. Reece stepped slowly through the doorway and let it close behind him. His eyes were on the man at the bottom of the steps.

"What can I help you with?"

Reece's tone sent a shiver through her. He stood straight, hands loosely at his sides, focused on the man in front of him. This was not the same person with whom she'd arrived or run inside from the rain. Reece's whole demeanor had changed.

The two men stared at each other. At the street, the taller of the two spat, said something, then threw a leg off his motorcycle. Reece's gaze flicked from the first man to the second. His head moved, and his look hardened before he shifted his gaze back to the first man. He lifted a brow.

The first man met his look, held it a moment, then threw a smirk in Kati's direction. "Just saying hello to the new babe. Maybe wondering who she belongs to?"

"She doesn't *belong* to anyone, but right now, she's with me."

The man nodded. His eyes studied Reece.

Reece moved closer, smiled. "But if you would like to stop by New Life Church this Sunday, you can meet your other neighbor, the assistant pastor there."

A laugh rose in the man's throat. Kati shivered again.

31

Lord...

"Assistant pastor? Yeah? And he lives here, too?" His voice included his friends in its merriment. "I might like to meet him. Someday." His focus slid to Kati again. His head dipped. He turned and walked back down the sidewalk.

The taller of the other two, obviously younger, said something. The first man spat out a sea of words in Spanish and mounted his bike. The younger man's head rose, his eyes on Reece. The skin over his face seemed to pull tight.

Another shudder went through Kati.

He mounted his bike. The three sent a roar of motors Kati and Reece's way and disappeared down the street.

"Thanks for the rescue," Kati managed.

Reece dropped his hand, clasped hers, and tugged her back inside. "Sit down, will you?" His voice carried the edge she'd heard earlier. He moved to the window. She stared. A gun stuck out from the back of his jeans, his T-shirt bunched behind it.

Her heart jumped. Just like at the gym. He'd had a gun that day, too. She dropped to the sofa. "You think they'll come back?"

"Circle the block and return? A possibility. I just want to make sure they don't. The leader, the one coming up here, liked what he saw when he saw you, but wasn't looking for a fight." He cast her an ironic smile. "The young one, now. Trouble."

Reece studied the street a few more minutes, then grabbed his keys from the end table. "Well, rain or not, bikers or not, let's go get those groceries for Mrs. Willis."

***

Kati smiled at the remembrance of that visit as she moved down the hospital corridor, heading back from lunch. "Miss Always Available for Ministry" would not be available at church today or tomorrow, so they'd have to make do without her. But she wouldn't miss this Wednesday evening's service. No, she'd make that for sure.

In the meantime, her volunteer day in the ER had started slow enough, but had picked up. The other RN, Carly, had mumbled a caution about the patient in 200, or was it his mother who might be a problem?

As she approached, voices came from behind the curtain. Spanish. Both angry. She put a smile on her face and slid the curtain open. The voices stopped.

Two people turned her way. Her patient, fourteen-year-old Martin Sanchez, and, if Carly was right, his mother. The boy's eyes were sunken, his face pale, but two red spots on his cheeks testified to the anger inside. His mother straightened and eyed her with relief.

"Hi," Kati said and introduced herself. "I'm here to get your medical information." She stepped to the hand sanitizer dispenser and cleansed her hands before moving to the boy's bedside. Her gaze traveled over him and rested on a laceration on his forearm. *Infected.* Perhaps a knife wound or something equally as sharp, not cutting, though. A defensive wound? Her interest jumped. Had the boy been in a fight? His arm rising to protect himself? As a fighter, she could see that.

Her gaze rose to meet his. The boy stared back, his eyes hard, challenging. Whatever had happened, he didn't look like he wanted to share it. Maybe if his mom left…

Kati shifted her scrutiny to the woman. "Hello."

"Hi." The woman stepped forward. "I'm so glad you're here. He thinks he'll be all right if he leaves. I told him that thing is infected and he has to have it looked at. Oh, I'm Josefina, his mother. Josey. Everyone calls me Josey. I have no idea how this happened." Her disgusted look at the boy said a lot. "He's not saying either, but it looks terrible, and he does too, and …" Her voice broke.

Kati nodded. Josey's hitched voice and her previous anger

LINDA K. RODANTE

gave Kati a clue as to the woman's concern. No matter his age, he was still her baby. Something had happened, and it had shaken her. A serious wound—for whatever reason left untreated and perhaps hidden. Kati tried the reassuring look she gave to frightened patients before she turned to Martin Sanchez.

"How are you feeling?"

"I'm fine." He threw another hard look at his mother.

"Okay. May I see your arm, please?"

The boy shrugged and held it up but grimaced with the movement. Kati took the arm to support it. He was obviously in pain no matter how much he wanted to deny it. And no wonder—between the color and the drainage, the whole look of it, the doctor would probably order a debridement along with blood work, antibiotic, and an MRI to check for osteomyelitis. And the boy might need a PICC—a pic line to administer the antibiotic right to the bloodstream.

Perhaps it wasn't as bad as she thought, but she wouldn't bet on it. Good thing the mother had brought him in.

She'd add them both to her prayer list.

Behind her, the mother scooted close. The boy's mouth straight lined. A wonder he wasn't scared. He had no idea how bad the wound looked nor the possible consequences if it was not treated quickly.

Lord, he's going to need you.

Kati glanced from the wound to Martin. "You're blessed to have such a caring mom."

The brown eyes slid to Josey and back. "Yeah."

"You're temperature is above 103." She wondered if he knew that was high. "Are you in pain?"

"No."

Josey made a noise in her throat. "Except you moaning all night long. I tell you, if I had seen this earlier—"

"Mamá."

Kati didn't understand his next words, but after a heated

34

back-and-forth in Spanish, he flopped back on the cot and stared at the ceiling.

"Please," Kati interrupted. "I need to get some information." She walked over to the electronic medical record computer. She could feel the mother's frustration and wondered how she'd react if a child of her own had this type of infection.

She caught the boy's attention. "Are you on any type of medicine or drugs, prescription or otherwise?"

"He better not be!" Josey's words jumped across the room. "We've talked about that. And the gangs. This…this wound better not be about any gang initiation or anything. I won't—"

The boy's voice interrupted her, and Kati wondered if she needed to ask the mother to step from the room. If the boy was using any illegal drugs, he certainly wouldn't tell her with his mother standing there.

Josey's phone rang, and she scrounged in her purse. "It's probably your sister. I texted her earlier."

"What? Why did you text her?" The boy leaned forward again. "Don't tell her nothing. Nada. You hear?"

Josey pulled the phone from her purse. "Of course I tell her. What do you think? We're at the hospital."

"No! Uncle Jerry will be here in no time."

"Of course he will. He's a cop. You think he wants you mixed up in some gang?" She turned away and began a rapid conversation in Spanish.

"I said it was an accident. An accident!"

"Yeah, yeah. Sure, I believe that. Mariana? You never guess where I'm at. The hospital. Yeah."

"Ma'am." Kati stepped forward and indicated the door. "Can you take the conversation outside, please?"

Josey shook her head at Martin and left the room. Her voice faded as the door closed behind her.

Kati looked at the boy. *I'm thinking boy. He's probably thinking he's a man.*

"You want to try this again, Martin? I need to know what meds or drugs you're on or have been taking so we can help you." She nodded at his arm. "You have a nasty cut there. It's infected. You're going to get some heavy-duty antibiotics here, so we need to know." She saw the hesitation. "With the HIPPA laws, I can try to keep this confidential, but we need to know."

He huffed. "I'm not on anything. Well, I found some of mom's old antibiotics and took those last week."

"What were they?"

"Something that started with an A…moxy something."

"Amoxicillin?"

"Yeah. I think so."

"Do you know how much? Five hundred milligrams, maybe?"

He shook his head.

"How often?"

"There were only four, so I just took one a day until they were gone."

"Nothing else?"

Martin hesitated.

She tilted her head. "We're in this to help you, Martin. We can't do that if you don't tell us the truth. Did you get any of your mother's pain meds?"

"Nah. She won't keep those. A…a friend gave me something."

Kati kept her face straight. "Okay. Do you remember the name of those?"

"Tram something. We joked about it. Trampoline, you know."

"Tramadol?"

"Yeah."

"How much were you taking?"

Through the rest of the questions and answers, Kati kept one ear on Josey's voice in the hall, glad that his mother obviously needed to vent to her daughter.

Time, Lord. I need time here. Help me minister to him.
The boy's description of his injury, the "accident" sounded concocted to her. He admitted to a knife wound. How it came about was another thing.

When she finally turned from the computer, the mother's voice had receded. Josey had maybe gone to find a bathroom.

Kati moved to the boy's bedside. "The doctor will be here soon. He'll order some blood work and start an antibiotic. He also might order a debridement. Do you know what that is?"

He shook his head.

"The infection is so acute that we'll need to remove anything that might promote infection, anything that would impede healing. We can use medicine, or perhaps we might have to cut away some of the skin and tissue."

The teen sucked in his breath, eyes rounding.

Kati nodded. "You'll probably be with us a few days. The doctor might also order an MRI just to make sure the infection is not in the bone. I don't know what happened, Martin, or what you're involved in, but this is serious. Left untreated, an infection can even end in death." All right, now she had his attention. "Whatever is going on in your life, your mother loves you. She's angry because she doesn't want anything to happen to you, and she's scared. Mothers are like that."

The boy grumbled under his breath, and Kati let her smile show. She pulled a small white book from her pocket. "I have a New Testament here. They're given out by the Gideons. Do you believe in God?"

"Sí."

"I thought you might. You're Catholic?"

"Sí."

"Well. This little book tells you about Jesus and why he came to earth. You've probably heard a lot about it before, but this book can be a real help. God is a real help. He's a very present help in trouble. You might be in trouble. I don't know, but I'm going to put this in your clothes bag. When you have time later, you can read it. I'll try to find one in Spanish if you want."

He shook his head. "No. This is fine."

"Okay. There are helps in this book. You can look in the front, where the Gideons have put the pages for certain verses that will help when you're in trouble or having a bad day. And just as we're trying to help you, your mother is trying to help, too. Even if she is upset with you right now. And your uncle, the cop?" She gave a soft chuckle at his grimace. "I'm sure he wants to help, too."

She paused before leaving. "And, Martin? God wants the best for you even more than we do. He's the real deal."

Chapter 3

And I sought for a man among them, that should make up the hedge, and stand in the gap before me
(Ezekiel 22:30 KJV)

On Wednesday, Kati scooted into church and into the pew at the last minute. The hospital had been filled today. People coming and going. The emergency room like a restaurant turn-around from morning to when she'd clocked out. She'd only had one chance to run to Martin's room and check on him. A man in uniform—deputy sheriff?—stood by the boy's bed. Both had been laughing when she pushed open the door. Warmth had filled her. She'd said hello, made some small talk about Martin's progress, then ducked out, almost colliding with his mom. Josey had a bag filled with some food that made Kati's stomach rumble as the scent rose to her nostrils. The boy was in good hands, and his prognosis looked good, too.

She settled back in the pew and looked around. Not many empty places. People packed the sanctuary tonight. Joshua's sermon and the aftermath had reached numerous ears. Tonight his prayer and his message had centered on 2 Corinthians 10:3–5. A familiar Scripture to her, and yet…

"How many realize that the Word of God is a weapon?" Joshua asked and peered across the sanctuary. Many raised their hands. "Which of you have used it today or this week to fight the Enemy?"

Fewer hands went up. He let the silence hang a moment.

"We've all lived so long with Satan's attacks that we no longer see them as such. Sickness, alcoholism, pornography, drug addiction, theft, rape, murder. These things are rampant today—perhaps in our lives personally—and yet we fight them with our own or society's solutions. We possess weapons of divine power that can demolish strongholds, and yet we don't use them.

"Prayer, praise, God's Word. The name of Jesus. Weapons. The Enemy can even keep you so busy you have no time to do God's work. Have we asked God for his discernment in our lives? Think about it. Next time you're sick or discouraged or afraid or worried, try praising God. Lift your voice. Thank him. Sing praises to him. God inhabits the praises of his people. Not because he needs it, but because we need it. His presence fills us with power and joy and awe. See if the depression or worry doesn't leave. Let it be a training ground into bigger warfare.

"I'm new here, so please listen carefully. I'm *not* saying stop taking your medicine or quit your counseling sessions. But I am asking you to search yourself. Where are you today, spiritually? Are you tired? Are you on the shelf? Would you like the fire of Christ in your life? Again or for the first time?"

He pointed upward, then to his chest. "It's up there and in here." He pointed out the back doors. "It's out there—in God's love for others, in the mission he's given us to accomplish. He's calling us out of our comfort zones, out of our safe zones, and asking if we are willing to take up the fight for our families, our neighbors, and for him."

He backed up from the podium. "Go home. Seek his face. Pray. See where God is leading you."

As the worship song began to play, Kati put her hands to her head and squeezed her eyes shut. His words had challenged her. Again. But her head felt like a swarm of gnats swirled inside. She didn't do headaches or migraines. What was this?

She forced her eyes open, and they focused on Ryann.

She'd come through the doors late and sat on the opposite side of the sanctuary. Kati's heart twinged. Their friendship had almost ceased to exist the last couple of months, timed with Ryann's declining attendance in church. All since Landon appeared on the scene.

Ryann rose and headed for the sanctuary doors. Her face looked haggard, and she'd never met Kati's eyes tonight.

Kati lurched to her feet and scrambled after her. She pushed open the church doors. The parking lot's light pole threw yellow light across the church porch. To her left and right cars pulled away and headed home. Which way had Ryann gone?

"Ryann!" She hurried down the steps.

China Osborne, her short, spiky hair almost a match for Kati's—except for the color—pointed to the right. "She took off that way. But you'll have to run if you want to catch her. She's outta here."

Reece stepped in front of her, and Kati sidestepped, her eyes on the parking lot.

"Kati." Reece caught her arm. "Don't go storming after her."

She threw him a surprised look. "I need to talk to her." The frustration inside was wound as tight as her boxing hand wraps.

"Maybe now is not the best time." His focus went over her head, and Kati twisted to see Ryann slip into her older-model Ford Mustang.

Kati tried to move past him, but Reece blocked her way again.

"She's my friend, Reece. You don't know her."

"And because of that, I might be a little more cautious about preaching to her."

"I wasn't going to preach."

He cocked his head. "Sure."

The Mustang's engine roared to life, and the car's exit left no doubt about the driver's attitude. Other cars eased out along the drive after her. The number of people coming from the sanctuary slowed. A couple glanced their way.

Kati dropped her head, then straightened. Why had the man interfered? "Who do you think you are, stopping me from talking with her?"

"You should have seen your face."

She clenched her fists. "You know why I took up kickboxing?"

"Because you like to knock people down?"

She narrowed her eyes and brought her fists up. "Because some of them deserve it."

He raised open hands in mock surrender. "No fighting here. I saw what you did to your trainer."

"Wimp." She feigned a right hook.

His arm jumped up for a block, but he dropped it. "My grandma always told me not to hit girls, but you're pushing it."

"Girls hit back these days, and you've got forty or fifty pounds on me and a few inches. Come on." Kati lifted her chin, bounced on her feet.

"Nope."

She glanced to where the Mustang had disappeared, dropped her fists, and sighed. Her heart ached. "I hate watching people throw their lives away."

Reece wrapped his arms around her waist and dragged her against him.

"Hey! Let go!"

"Just wanted to get past those fists of yours."

She squirmed and shoved against his chest.

"What's going on here? Someone need rescuing?" Joshua's voice came from the sanctuary doors. Kati heard the key turn in the lock, and he bounded down the steps. Reece dropped his arms.

"I'm glad you finally showed, bro." Reece laced his words with mock concern. "I might have needed 911 if you hadn't appeared. The girl's always ready for a fight."

"Oh right, and you're not playing hand-to-hand combat?" Kati turned to Joshua. "I wanted to talk with Ryann. You know, the friend I introduced you to the other day? But the beast here"—she pointed at Reece—"kept me from it."

"Oh?" The men's eyes met over her head.

Talk about feeling left out. What was up?

"Yes, *oh*."

Josh glanced down. "Perhaps because he knew I'd spoken with her earlier."

"To Ryann?"

"She called today. Dropped by my office."

Kati waited, but he said nothing more. "Okay. Privileged information. But I'm glad she came." She huffed a breath. "I guess I didn't need to go 'storming after her' then."

Reece's mouth hitched, and Kati gave a quick shake of her head. She'd enjoyed the time she'd spent with him at Mrs. Willis'. The man had acted as if he were the lady's grandson—asking if she needed anything, fetching her coffee from the kitchen, helping her rise when they left. He had as many facets to his character as a marquise diamond.

Joshua shot a look around the parking lot. "You're heading home? I'm bushed, and we're leaving, but I don't want you here alone."

"I'm feeling the same way. It's been a long day." Kati ran a hand through her short hair, feeling the tiredness. Sparring with Reece was as bad as sparring with Terry. Different, but still exhausting. His arms around her had oozed strength though. His chest hard and muscled. She shook herself.

"Let me walk you to your car, Kate." Josh broke into her thoughts.

"No need, Pastor. It's right here." She threw him a smile, waved briefly to Reece, and headed to the car parked nearby.

Joshua followed behind and opened her door. "Not locked? I know you can protect yourself, but take precautions, Kate. We've invited the neighborhood in, and some of them might bear watching."

She slipped behind the wheel. How well she knew that. She looked back at Reece. He'd moved to his SUV nearby. Reece's stockier, broad-shouldered look contrasted with Joshua's lean, wiry build. Handsome men, she thought. More in the way they carried themselves and in their eyes and the lines of their mouths. They were caring men, Kati decided. That was what made them handsome.

***

Josh leaned back in the SUV, glad, as usual, that he wasn't driving. When the tiredness hit like it did now, he didn't want to be behind the wheel. His days usually started with prayer and Bible study at 4:45 AM, and the evenings went on too late sometimes.

He turned his head. "Anything going on back there I should know about?"

Reece kept his eyes on the road. "No. I was trying to stop her from laying into Ryann, and she came at me with her fists."

"I told you to be on good behavior around her."

"She was joking."

"Hmm…but your manhood felt threatened enough that you put her in a bear hug?"

Reece sent him a sideways glance. "Just getting under her defenses. Momentarily."

"Hmm…"

"Give me a break, Josh. Nothing's going on there. I hardly know the woman."

"Good. Because we have enough to concentrate on with Ryann and her boyfriend and the gang members. You're sure they were gang members?"

"Yes. Diamonds on their jackets, colors on their backs. I couldn't get a good look at those. Nothing escalated, but you know this was what I warned you about. You go into neighborhoods like this, and you can expect trouble. I didn't like the fact that he honed in on Kati so fast."

"Me either. Keep her away from the house."

"I'd already decided that."

"We're getting with the Sheriff's Office this week, and Rich Richards will join us."

"*We*? I told you I'm not heading up any security team."

Joshua leaned his head back against the seat. "You were paid to do it back home, but you won't do it here?"

"That was different. I knew who the bad guys were. Here? No."

"You know one."

"The kid at the gym?"

"Yeah. Why didn't you tell the police you could identify him? You got a good look at him, didn't you?"

"I looked at their online books. He wasn't there."

Josh threw him a look. "But he was one of the three that showed at our place when Kati was there."

Reece shrugged.

"And he recognized you?"

"Pretty sure."

"Reece—"

"Just trying to get a feel of the land before I cause any trouble."

Joshua frowned. "Okay. I don't know how all this works. You do. Which is why I need your expertise with the security team at the church."

"Why do I feel like Watson to your Sherlock? Getting dragged into things? Things I'd left behind."

"You're getting dragged along, bro, because you're hesitating in the doorway. It's time to jump out the door." His gaze slid to his friend. "Like you told me when you first took me skydiving. Just jump."

Reece made a noise in this throat.

"Besides, you keep me from taking myself too seriously."

Joshua closed his eyes. "I need your balance."

"Well, you won't have me forever. I'm almost thirty-three years old. Jesus had finished his ministry by then. I haven't found mine yet, but when I do..."

"I know. You're out of here."

"I can't be Watson forever. Or is it Spock? Second-in-command."

Joshua straightened, shifted. "You've never been second, Reece. You're your own person, and that person is always number one in God's sight—and in mine."

"This conversation is getting sappy. Go to sleep. I'll wake you when we get to the house."

Joshua yawned. "Or we could talk about the attractive woman you had in your arms earlier."

"Hot. The word is hot." He shook his head. "Go to sleep."

Joshua grinned and let the noise from the air conditioner wash all thoughts of hot women and Sherlock Holmes from his mind.

***

Kati climbed out of the car. Days at work were always long, but today especially so. She threw her lunch bag onto the counter and headed for bed. Hours later, she dragged herself out and down the hall. Fatigue, mixed with a lingering depression from something she couldn't identify, edged her vision. She wandered to the kitchen, made herself a cup of Darjeeling tea, and sat at the table.

What was her problem? Joshua had thrown a challenge at them—no, God had—and she couldn't seem to scrape herself off the floor to consider it.

The tea's aroma lifted to her nostrils. She took a sip, sat back. *I can't be that tired. And what do I have to be depressed about? Why so down?*

Of course, the way Ryann's life was headed had discouraged Kati for a while. Someone so on fire for God now barely making it to church and not returning calls… *What is going on there, Lord?* How could this guy draw Ryann away from everything she'd cared about?

And then Reece—with a gun. And not just having a gun, but the way he carried it, with familiarity. And his demeanor when he'd stepped onto the porch the other day, as scary as the men on the motorcycles.

His tattoos. All right, everyone had tattoos these days, but Reece had quite a few. None on his face or neck, but on his forearms, others on his upper arms and shoulders, from what she'd seen when he wore a short-sleeved shirt—which he did most days. He didn't try to hide them. She chewed her lip a minute. He didn't try to display them either.

Is this what we prayed for, Lord? Her mind whirled. She and Miss Eleanor and the others in the prayer group had prayed for God to do something radical. And this felt radical.

So if it was God, what was she going to do about it? She was so fed up with not having what people called "the courage of her convictions" and of wondering what they would all say if they knew the truth. Could she find the courage to do what Joshua was asking?

God had told the Israelites that he was giving them a land filled with milk and honey, but then he told them to go in and possess it. Wow. That wasn't usually what you thought when you heard of God's gifts. In this instance, you actually had to work for them—or, rather, battle for them. She mulled that over in her mind.

Sometimes God told the people to watch his salvation. Stand still and see the salvation of the Lord. But sometimes he'd told them to go in and possess the land. Other translations said "go in and *take* it." Take it. Joshua wasn't calling them to battle; God was.

So her tiredness, her depression, her uncertainty—all from the devil. It certainly wasn't from God. She'd been so under

47

attack that she hadn't recognized it for what it was.

And if she was depressed, then what other members had a similar problem? She was calling Miss Eleanor right now. She needed a prayer partner.

***

On Sunday Joshua noticed the increase in attendance. He hadn't thought about it. He knew some would leave as the changes started and others would come from outside. Numbers didn't matter. He wanted Navy SEALs. His mouth hitched, and he wondered if he should say that. He shook his head. *Keep me out of this, Lord. Say what you want, and don't let me get in the way.*

The praise and worship lifted his soul. He wanted to kneel. Wondered what the congregation would think about it, then did it anyway. Knelt down, dropped his head. *God, I run to you. Fill me with your presence and love, with all that I need today, with what you want.*

After a few minutes, he stood. Others in the congregation still worshipped. Kati's arms and head were lifted, her eyes closed. He smiled and let his eyes wander to the other worshippers. Reece stood at the back, but his eyes were closed, too.

Joshua's heart enlarged. The Lord's arms were open.

He stepped up to podium. He let the words ease out, trying not to upset the move of the Holy Spirit across the sanctuary. It was always a tightrope, feeling his way, trying to decide if what he was about to say was what God wanted him to, or was it just him?

"You know the parable where a man's friends tore up the roof to lower him down to Jesus? And Jesus forgave the man's sins and healed him? Well, the verse above those verses, John 5:17, states that the religious leaders and others were gathered together to hear Jesus teach and that *the power of the Lord was present to heal them.* God was present, his power was present, but it's only recorded that this one person was healed. The Scripture says the power of the Lord was present to heal *them*. In other words, more than one person could have been healed that day. But the religious leaders were indignant that Jesus forgave the man his sins.

"Do we miss God because of the way we think things should be? I believe God is here, now, and that he wants to move in our lives. Will we let him?" Joshua paused a moment. "Let me say something more. When I heard of the opening here for an assistant pastor, God grabbed my heart—almost as if it was wrenched out of me. And I'm sure God didn't bring me here for church as usual. We don't need church as usual.

"Many of you have met Reece Jernigan by now. He doesn't say a whole lot when you first meet him, but I bet you all have a feeling for the type of man he is. Reece has been in the trenches ministering for three years. He dragged me along with him. Now, I've dragged him here. We've come to wrench you out of your comfort zones, to call you to battle.

"People outside these doors are dying. We're going to reach them. We're going to war. I'm calling you to prayer—at home and here. Then we're going into the highways and the byways to compel them to come in."

***

Reece waved her toward his SUV. "I don't argue with the boss. Do you?"

Kati growled in her throat. Apparently being called into battle didn't apply to her. When Joshua had found out where she was headed, he'd assigned her a bodyguard. "If I'd left from my house, what would you—and he—have done? Nothing! Because you'd have never known."

"That's just it. You aren't leaving from your house, and the fact that Terry's temporary gym is close to the same neighborhood as before has left Josh...protective."

49

"I don't need a babysitter."

"No, but think of it this way—I'm riding shotgun in case you need one."

She huffed. "This is stupid."

"Might be, but I kind of laid into him the other day. He's planned this 'Get to Know the New Assistant Pastor' party for this next weekend. Sent out three hundred invitations to addresses around the church, and I told him it might bring the kind of attention—and neighbors—he didn't want. So, now he's on the offense, and that includes you today."

Kati climbed into the passenger seat under his outstretched arm. He closed the door and moved around to the driver's side.

"So…"

She jerked her head in his direction. "So, okay. I'll let you do this. This once. I don't need you to babysit me back and forth to my class. That's why I took kickboxing, anyway."

"So you could knock people around?"

"Will you stop? If I need self-defense, I know it."

"Trust me, kickboxing or not, you don't want to tangle with those guys. Ever."

She stared at the scenery, thinking. "He's right, you know."

"Josh? Yeah, he has a habit of that. Being right."

"I mean, inviting the neighborhood. Getting the prayer meeting going. Talking about prayer-walking the neighborhood."

"I said he was right most of the time. Doesn't mean I agree with all he's doing."

"But reaching out to those that don't know God, don't believe in Jesus. That's what we're about, isn't it?"

"I hear this from him all the time."

"Well?"

"Of course it is. Doesn't make my job any easier, though."

"What is your job, Reece?"

He laughed. "Got you there, don't I? Ms. RN."

"I'll just ask Joshua."

"He doesn't know what I do."

"What does that mean?"

"He thinks he does. He thinks God's placed me alongside him to help with the vision he has. And that might be true to an extent, but"—he stopped, glanced her way—"that's not all."

"Hmm…"

"He has a death wish. He'll walk up to anyone and start preaching, and I mean anyone. If he'd been there on the porch with us the other day, he wouldn't have gone to get a gun. He'd have gotten his Bible."

"You did get your gun. I saw it."

"I know. I had put it away that day. Stupid. It will be with me from now on."

Her heart jumped. "You have it now?"

He nodded. "Don't worry. I'm not thinking I'll need it, but from now on, I'll err on the side of safety."

He pulled into the parking lot. "How long do you work out?"

"An hour or two."

"Mind if I wait?"

She opened the door before he could get around to her side. She grinned as he frowned at her.

"Who brought you up, Reece?"

"My grandmother. Why?"

She slid him an amused look. "Just wondered."

"Who brought you up, Ms. Walsh?"

She ducked her head and walked into the building. The familiar sounds of punching—the thumps, thwacks, shoops—along with the grunts, deep breaths, and exhales—pumped her adrenaline. She headed across the gym to warm up.

What was it with these guys, anyway? First Joshua and now Reece? Why the concern about her family? Yeah, she'd asked about his, but… Her look caught Reece's where he'd stopped near the back of the gym. She twisted away.

Terry walked by and gave her a nod. "Some sparring later?"

"Maybe."

"I haven't seen you as much the last couple of weeks." He indicated Reece with a tilt of his head. "Been busy?"

"I have been busy, but not what you're thinking. He's just a friend that brought me."

"A friend now? From stranger to friend. Maybe he'd like to join us. Use your friend pass, and he can work out."

"Maybe I will."

Before she headed to the punching bags, she made her way over to Reece.

"Have you boxed before? Would you like to work out? I have a friend pass."

Reece shook his head. "Thanks, but I'll just wait here."

"Afraid I'll take advantage of you?"

He grinned. "Afraid you'd get me with that roundhouse kick of yours."

She bounced on her feet. "Oh, come on. I'll let you spar with the bags then."

He shook his head. "Sorry."

"Well, Terry wants another round."

Reece frowned. "I thought all this kickboxing was about getting into shape and *maybe* using it if you needed. What's with the sparring? You're not a boxer."

"No, but Terry thought it would help me hone my skills."

"It seemed you honed them on him last time."

She couldn't help the grin. "He wasn't happy, was he?"

"And that's a problem when you're sparring. You learn to control your anger in a fight, or you've lost it. In most cases."

"Talking from experience, Reece?"

His head lowered. "Just talking, Ms. Walsh."

She feigned a right hook as she had the other night, but this time he didn't move. "Okay. I'll go put in some time with the bags, then take Terry up on his offer."

Reece's frown returned. "Don't make him mad, Lady

Walsh, or you might not win so easily this time."

"You just said if he gets angry, he'll lose."

"I said in most cases."

***

Reece stood near a corner of the ring, glad to see that both Kati and Terry had put on body protectors. A number of other fighters or members gathered to watch, too.

Terry gave a short introduction, and then he and Kati eased into it, doing a slow dance, with jabs, hooks, uppercuts, and kicks. Terry was going through a series of moves, classic combinations. Repeating them for the onlookers.

Jab, jab, low right hand. Repeat. And then again.

Jab, straight right, left hook, roundhouse kick. Repeat. Again.

Left hook kick, jab, straight right hand, right foot jab. Repeat. Again.

Jab, right hand, right hook kick, left back kick. Repeat. Again.

Kati parried each one. They'd done this before.

She was good. Quick, responsive, and she knew the moves, but Terry had years of practice behind him. The lucky uppercut that Kati had downed him with last time was just that. Lucky. It didn't take much to see that, nor to see how Terry liked showing off before an audience.

Reece noticed when the dance changed, when the tempo jumped. It took Kati a second beat to catch it. The sparring had begun.

Terry threw a roundhouse kick to her body—quicker and more powerful than those he'd thrown before. She brought her knee up to defend, but left her head open. His second one went to her head. She parried but kept her arm up this time. Terry caught the roundhouse she sent his way and threw it, coming in with another kick himself. Laughter came from the men in the crowd. The few women egged Kati on.

The timing changed again, but as Terry threw another kick to her head, she evaded, then caught his jab and countered it. The tittering among the crowd didn't bode well for her. Terry sent a power punch to her face, but she stopped it with a push kick to his hip. Reece's jaw tightened. They weren't wearing head protection—which was why Kati's uppercut had decked Terry before. No one needed a power punch to the face in a sparring match.

Kati threw a new combination, which Terry countered and evaded. However, the trainer hadn't expected his student to take the advantage. His next combination—a jab, right hand, low left hook—were all quick and powerful and caused Kati to reel back.

Laughs, whistles, and guffaws made Reece grimace. With a grin, Terry stepped back to give her some time. She frowned, clearly not liking his grin or the obvious time he'd given, as if she needed it. Reece shook his head. She was too easy to read, and Terry should know right now that she was coming for him. Perhaps he was a little cocky. When she threw another new combination, she caught him by surprise again. His grin wavered.

Low laughter came from the viewers, and his next move was to put her in her place. Axe kick, jab, switch kick—with the axe kick barely missing her face. Terry had gauged it to do that, but Reece still didn't like it. Kati was in over her head and starting to slow.

"Take a break," Terry said and turned away.

Kati backed toward the corner. Reece strode over and grabbed her towel.

"Kati."

She turned, and he waved the towel. She moved closer. He reached up and wiped the sweat from her face, grabbed her water bottle, and lifted it to her mouth. She drank greedily. He waited until she finished.

"Kati, you're tired. End this."

She shook her head. "I have to let him get some cred back from the other day."

Reece bit back an expletive. "That's ridiculous. Anyway, he's got that. He's pushing for more."

"Kati, you up for this?" Terry's voice taunted. "Or does your boyfriend want to take your place?"

The boil inside hit Reece with surprise. Man, he'd love to take her place, show this guy just what being a punching bag felt like.

Kati straightened.

Reece grabbed her arm. "Okay. Listen. You're tired. Your kicks are slowing. Throw a knee instead. And use the jab more. Keep him at bay. And keep your gloves up. You're dropping them. And, Kati, now's not the time to make him mad."

She gave a twisted smile. "All right."

"There's no humiliation in ending this. It's a sparring match, not a competition."

She nodded and moved toward the center with a lot less bounce than Reece wanted to see. He growled when the other man grinned. A sparring match. They weren't even wearing headgear.

***

The streetlight covering the church parking lot couldn't hide her exhaustion, any more than the ride home could. She'd tried bluffing her way through at first, but when he'd insisted she "put her head back, shut up, and rest," she did just that.

He stood by the driver's door of her car now. When she leaned over to drop her duffel bag into the backseat, he forced his eyes away from the tight leggings. He'd had to do that more than once tonight. Something he found hard, but something Josh had taught him—not to leer at women anymore. He closed his eyes. That part of his former self still had to be conquered.

55

The other men who gathered for the sparring match hadn't worried about it, though. Reece had noticed their ogling—which bothered him as much as Terry using her for a punching bag. He wondered if she knew or cared. Her other attire, what he'd seen so far, fit modestly enough.

"The guys at the gym liked watching the match."

She stopped, rolling the key fob in her hand. "Yeah, they seem to. Always come around when Terry and I are sparring. Reece, you seemed pretty familiar with the fighting—"

"They liked watching you."

Her face stilled for a moment, and he wondered if she was processing what he'd said.

"Is that good or bad?"

It bothered him more than it should. "Depends on how you look at it."

"What are you saying?"

He hesitated. "Between them watching you get beat on and the tight clothes, well, some guys get off on that. Just watch yourself." Okay, he'd said what he wanted to, covered the part that had caused him unease. He stepped back.

She hesitated a moment, chewing on her lip. "Okay. Listen, where did you learn to box?"

"Tell me about your parents."

Her face changed, and she opened the car door. He caught it before she could close it. "We both have things we hide."

She punched the starter and met his look. "Maybe."

"There are no maybes here, Battle Maiden." The irritation showed in her face, and he chuckled. "The name suits you."

"You've given me a couple of names, and I'm not sure I like any of them."

He reached through the window and touched her cheek. "Maybe I'll find one you do." He dropped his hand and stepped away.

Her lips parted as if to say something, but then confusion kaleidoscoped across her face. She looked away, put the car in reverse, and backed out.

He stared after her and sought to control his own bewilderment. He'd wanted to touch her all evening, hadn't realized what it was until now, hadn't grasped why the other guys' smirks had disturbed him. No, as Joshua had said earlier, they had too much going on for anything like this.

This was not good.

Chapter 4

But I say unto you, love your enemies, bless them that curse
you, do good to them that hate you, and pray for them which
despitefully use you, and persecute you.
(Matthew 5:44 KJV)

Joshua stopped gathering the papers from his desk and turned to Kati. "You're sure you don't mind playing administrative assistant for this security meeting? Is that the correct term nowadays? Is it administrative coordinator? Or executive something?"

"I'm not concerned with the title. Call me whatever feels right."

"You're a blessing, you know that? Easy to work with. And you see things—the little things I miss, the people I miss."

"That's because I know the people. You will after a time."

He smiled, shoved the rest of the papers in a file folder, and handed it to Kati. "I probably won't need any of this, but…"

"'But' is right. Someone will ask something that you don't have the answer to, but we'll know it's in here somewhere."

Kati tucked the file folder into what looked like an over-sized handbag. As long as it was all there… He took a deep breath and grinned. She'd been a world of help over these past few weeks. Her thinking matched his in a lot of ways. Different from China Osborne, the secretary who met with him in his office every morning.

China had begun helping Pastor Alan about six months ago, and she was great with the computer and technical stuff, but she couldn't seem to grasp the vision he had. He'd heard her cautions and listened to some skeptical words as she tried to get him to wait upon doing anything until Alan returned. Funny, but Alan told him to forge ahead with what God had laid on his heart, because he and Daneen needed extra time to settle his brother's estate.

"I have perfect faith in you, Josh, or I wouldn't have hired you. And I have faith in God. He sent you and your friend Reece. I see a kind of David and Jonathan there. There's nothing you can do that we cannot work through or around—or embrace—when I get back."

Freedom. That was what the man released into him. Freedom to do what he felt God leading him to do.

His eyes focused. Kati stood nearby, a small smile on her face. "You there, Pastor?"

Yeah, he was here and glad she was, too. He started to reach out a hand, to tell her how much her smile encouraged him, but he stopped himself just in time. Getting too personal too soon was not what he needed. "I'm here. Let's go. Another official duty faced—and hopefully conquered in a few hours." He ushered her through the doorway. "That is if Mrs. Clemson doesn't put up too much of a disturbance."

***

Church members and other people Joshua didn't recognize had crammed the Life Center. He stood at one end, microphone clipped to his open-necked shirt. Casual tonight. It was how he'd planned it. Security meeting, no tension, casual. Only Mrs. Clemson was trying hard to hold up the play—or rather had blocked all their efforts to proceed.

Reece leaned against the back wall, arms crossed, not bothering to conceal his amusement. Josh narrowed his eyes at him, which only caused Reece's grin to widen.

He turned his attention back to the woman standing in front of him and her specific question about safety during the prayer walk. She'd stepped close, almost in his face. He'd like to put some space between them, but that might look like retreat, and he wasn't retreating.

"Yes, Mrs. Clemson, that is what this meeting is about. That's why we have Detective Richards and the US Coast Guard, in the form of Jake Osborne, as well as a deputy from the Sheriff's Office all in attendance."

"Well, let me put it this way, young man. How can anyone plan on being safe when they are determined to run into the fire—as you seem so determined to do with this prayer walk in the north-side neighborhood? And we all know what that neighborhood is like."

Her "young man" sounded like she'd been a school principal and was about to wield a long-outdated paddle. When Miss Eleanor had used the same term earlier, he'd found it mildly humorous, but then he knew she was for him. He'd known when he accepted the position that his age would be an obstacle he'd have to climb. In fact, in one of their many phone conversations, Pastor Alan had served up 1 Timothy 4:12 to him—"Don't let anyone despise you because you are young."

Kati stepped forward. "You know, Clarice, that is exactly what *firemen* do. They run into the fire—to save people. But they train first, prepare themselves. That's what Pastor Josh wants us to do. To prepare ourselves. And this meeting is a first step."

Joshua winced. Not quite true. The security team had met three times already. But this was a first step for the congregation.

Rich Richards cleared his throat. "What we have explained tonight—the establishment of a security team, the installation of new locks and monitoring equipment, even the bulletproofing of the podium and pews, thanks to an undisclosed donor, are first steps in security for the church. And they are good steps. Whether the congregation does or does not go into the north-side neighborhood is beside the point. In today's society, we must take these steps, but nothing we do is foolproof."

The woman's hands shot into the air. "That's exactly what I'm saying. Why ask for trouble when there's enough out there as it is? You're putting people in harm's way."

China tilted her head at him. Her words earlier in the day had been the same. Joshua drew a deep breath. Maybe the fact that her husband risked his life each day to save people lost at sea was all she could handle.

In the back, Pedro Gonzalez stood. "Señor Josh, may I speak?"

"Certainly, Pedro. I welcome all comments and questions." Well, he'd told himself he would anyway. As if Reece could read his mind, Josh noticed his friend's grin again. *Yeah, have a good time, bro. Enjoy it. One day you'll be on this end.*

Pedro turned in all directions, letting his gaze travel over those in the Life Center before facing Joshua again. "Gloria a Dios."

"Gloria a Dios," the woman next to him repeated. "Glory to God." She was big with child, her dark hair curling around her shoulders, her eyes flashing in anger.

Joshua glanced from her back to Pedro. Anger? And then the knowledge of why washed through him. Where had he been? So focused on protecting himself that he'd failed to see them and others—the others he hadn't recognized by name or face—in their midst. *Oh, God, forgive me.*

Pedro nodded, as if seeing Joshua's realization. "Most of you know Pastor Alan hired me when no one else would. I've been here four years. Maria's been here one." He indicated the woman next to him with a tilt of his head. "You attended our wedding, were happy for us. I consider you amigos and hermanos. And yet hearing you talk—a knife has been placed in my heart. Are Maria and I so different from you? Are you scared of us? Do you not know where we live? Have you not visited our house? It is three houses down from Señor Josh and Señor Reece. Why do you think that if you come into our neighborhood that we will come to the church and kill you?" Any noise dropped away. No one moved. "Are those in our neighborhood not worthy of your love and concern? Where is this Christianity you talk about? Is it only for you? Your family and no one else? Or is it for everyone, as Jesus has said?"

He sat down. Maria glanced around again, sniffed, and sat next to him.

Joshua closed his eyes. He had no words to follow that. *Father, please talk to each one of us.*

Someone else cleared their throat. Josh opened his eyes. Miss Eleanor stood near the middle of the room. He nodded in her direction.

"I think, Pastor Josh, that Pedro has given us a lot to pray about. This might be a good time to close this meeting so we can go home do just that."

Joshua smiled. "I agree. And thank you, Pedro, for reminding us what this is all about."

***

Reece stepped into the doorway of Josh's office. "It was a good meeting."

Joshua rolled his eyes. A mix of excitement and tightrope walking swirled inside. "I thought Mrs. Clemson would torpedo us, but…"

"But Pedro…" Kati dumped her bag on Joshua's desk. "But Pedro…Actually, we have lots of support. A number of people already asked me about taking part in the prayer walk."

Joshua caught Reece's attention and nodded toward Kati. "She sees positive when I'm still reeling from the darts thrown."

"Give it up, Josh. You know victory when you see it. That was victory."

He couldn't help the grin. "It's falling into place. It's coming together."

"Did you think it wouldn't?"

"There are times, you know, when I question, just like you or anyone else." He stretched but kept a studied eye on Reece. The man was part of this vision. For some reason, Reece thought he was on the outside, but Joshua knew better. God had Reece here for a reason. The certainty wouldn't leave him.

"I'm excited!" Kati's enthusiasm encompassed them, and they all grinned.

Then Reece sobered. "Well, I'm heading out. I'll leave you to walk the young lady to her car, Josh. You'll have to drive yourself home."

"I know. My car's here, and I think the adrenaline will keep me going tonight. Kate? You ready to go?"

Her head swung Reece's way, hesitated, and then she nodded. "Yes, I'm bushed. But let me put away the papers first." She reached for her oversized bag.

Reece slipped from the room, and Josh grabbed his keys. "Could you leave them for tomorrow? I'll have China straighten them out, and I promise to get your bag back to you."

She hesitated again. "You're sure? I don't know how China will like that."

"She's fine. She'll love to see what you and I got up to anyway. I have the feeling she likes being in on things."

"Well, there's nothing in there she didn't hear about tonight."

"Exactly, but she can see that for herself." He gave a lopsided smile and ushered her out. The sooner he got home, the sooner he'd get some sleep. He locked the door, and they headed for the parking lot.

The moonlight softened the yellow lights as they crossed the parking lot. It highlighted her blonde hair. He had the urge to take her arm but quenched it. That urge had presented itself a number of times lately. He needed to watch it, needed to keep focused on what God was instructing him to do, not on the lady beside him.

The roar of a motorcycle sounded nearby. Joshua glanced around. Reece had disappeared quickly, and so had everyone else. He picked up his pace. "Climb in the car, will you?"

Kati slipped in, and he closed the door.

"Just stay here if they pull up. Don't open the door. Don't get out."

A lone Harley swerved into the parking lot, shot across it, and slid to a stop in front of Joshua. The man planted both feet on either side of the bike. Joshua began a silent prayer. His gaze took in the man's jacket and tattoos. Their eyes were at the same level. A tall man.

Joshua stepped forward. "Hi. Can I help you with something?"

The man took his time answering. He studied the parking lot for a moment, then brought his gaze back to Joshua.

"I heard you had a meeting tonight."

"Yes, we did."

"Something about security."

"Right again."

The man sat back on his bike. "The only security you're gonna find is with us."

Joshua nodded. "Who is *us*?"

"The Soldiers to you."

"The Soldiers?"

"Yeah? You heard of us?"

"I'm sorry. I haven't."

The man stood again. Even in the yellow light, Josh could see his eyes narrow.

"You that new pastor?"

"The assistant pastor, yes. And yes, I'm new."

"Where's your friend?"

Joshua's chest tightened. Was he talking about Kati? Had he waited, somewhere, watching until everyone left? "What friend?"

"Your brother, man. The one with the 'tude. Where is he?"

Joshua shrugged, relief warring with caution. The man didn't know Kati was here. Now if he could keep it that way. "He left a while ago."

"You tell him he ain't safe in that house of his. And you ain't safe either. Unless we allow it. You got that?"

"I'm pretty sure I understand what you're saying, but we're not here to cause any problems. We're just here—"

"I know why you're here, fundie. And now you know why I'm here." He revved the motorcycle. "I'll be back."

Joshua stood still while the bike swerved past him and headed down the street. Strange. Reece had said there were three before. Would a leader come on his own to issue a threat? Or was this someone else? Someone who had set fire to a gym? His insides tightened.

He jerked around when he heard a sound behind him. Kati stood next to her car. "I saw him leave."

Concern welled in him again, and he stepped to her side. "I don't think he knew you were here."

The wind tossed her short hair, and her eyes, even in the dim light, showed alarm. He put an arm around her and gave her a squeeze. "You're okay, Kate."

"I know. It's just a surprise to have him come out of the dark like that."

"Yeah, but I think it was a chance encounter. He couldn't have been watching us, or he'd have known you were here."

"That makes sense. It's amazing how brave I think I am when I'm kickboxing, but just now…"

He laughed and dropped his arm. She didn't move away. Instead, she shivered, and he squelched the urge to pull her to him again. "We all feel that way."

"You looked fine to me."

"Did I? Shaking in my boots, I promise you."

"Yeah, why don't I believe you?"

"You should." He took a deep breath. "Reece worries about this particular thing. I do, too. For others. For you." He looked down at her and brushed the wind-blown hair from her eyes. Surprise shot through him at the warm softness of her skin.

"But not for yourself?"

He hesitated then shrugged. "I can't say I don't, but it's different. People matter more than I do."

"That's admirable." She lifted her head, her smile filling him with warmth.

Whoa. He stepped back. "I'm not admirable. God is. *He* put something inside me. His love for others."

"Of course."

He opened her car door. "Why aren't you married, Kate? Or at least dating?"

"Oh, well…"

"Sorry. Nosy, aren't I?"

"No. It's okay. There's just never been anyone. Well, no one like that. Right now, it's just me and God. And that's okay."

"That's the way I feel. When he brings that special person, I'll know. At least I think I will. In the meantime…"

The wind played in her hair again, and something stirred inside him. His eyes dropped to her mouth. Her lips parted slightly. He swallowed and steeled himself against their pull. "You'd better get some rest, Kate, or you'll be looking for a chauffeur like mine."

"Only he left you tonight."

"Yeah. Of all nights. Get in, will you? I'll follow you down the drive."

She slid into her car. He climbed into his and pulled out behind her. When she turned onto the main road, he kept his foot on the brake and stared after her.

"At least I think I will," he muttered. "Lord, what just happened there? She's special, yes, but… There's no way I need a woman in my life right now. Is this you, or do I need to fight the Enemy here?" He put the car in drive and pulled out onto the highway.

Whatever it was, it was not good.

***

Kati threw the blanket back from her bed, slipped out, and padded to the window. The moonlight seemed brighter than a few hours before, brighter than when she'd stood looking up at Joshua, brighter than when his gaze had dropped to her mouth.

She wrapped her arms around herself and felt Reece's arms from a week before, felt the touch of his finger along her cheek the other night.

She shook herself. Wow. After so long. Two men. Two men who interested her, who attracted her. She should be dancing for joy, and as she thought about the surprised looks on both their faces, she couldn't help a smile. She bit her lip, and the smile faded.

She liked them both. They were admirable in different ways, and each stirred feelings she hadn't felt for a long time. But if they knew her, if they knew what a coward she was, would they feel the same? If they knew how she'd fled her home, if they knew why…

Lord, I'm trying to get my feet back under me. You know that.

She studied the moon-tossed shadows, noted the way the trees and lawn were edged with gold. She'd bought the house with the money she'd received, bought it for the large back-yard, the tall trees, the privacy. Her bedroom looked out onto the deck and the trees beyond. She sighed. Peace was what she'd come here for. Only God had drawn her out of herself this last year, giving her a hunger for the things he wanted. A hunger she had buried too long.

She turned and stepped away from the window.

But, Lord, they're friends, close friends. I can't cause a problem between them. I won't. Please help in this situation. This...is not good.

Chapter 5

In the same way, the Spirit helps us in our weakness. We do not know what we ought to pray for, but the Spirit himself intercedes for us through wordless groans. And he who searches our hearts knows the mind of the Spirit, because the Spirit intercedes for God's people in accordance with the will of God. (Romans 8:26–27 NIV)

Y ou volunteered for this, right?" Reece insisted.

Kati had stayed away from the church office and Joshua and Reece for a week, but when the call went out for volunteers for the upcoming "Get to Know the New Assistant Pastor" get-together, she couldn't help but come.

"Yes, but—"

"The three hundred invitations reached the neighborhood. We got ours. That was a waste of a good stamp. So, now we need food to feed whoever shows. And Josh assigned that to me. And you, Miss Warrior, are the only one here this afternoon. Mush."

"Don't 'mush' me. I'm not a dog. Or a warrior either."

He opened the church office door and ushered her out. "You're definitely a warrior."

"Your names for people—" She stopped in front of his SUV, hands on hips.

"Just get in the car. Two of us grabbing groceries will make it faster. You get the bakery items on the list and the produce. I'll grab the rest of the stuff."

She slipped into the seat and snapped the seat belt closed and glared at him. But truth was, him calling her a warrior didn't feel bad.

"So, let's go over the food list, Your Majesty."

His mouth spread in that grin she'd come to recognize, and she rolled her eyes.

Less than an hour later, they hefted bags of groceries into the back of his black Range Rover Sport. Kati searched in the bags until she found the box of cookies she'd bought for herself and opened them before she climbed into the front seat.

Sugar cookies with sprinkles. She couldn't help it if she'd never grown out of her love for them. They crunched in her mouth, and the sweetness rolled in. She offered one to Reece, who shook his head. She pulled another from the bakery box and another and another.

His head twisted her way, and Kati stopped with her hand halfway to her mouth. "It's just the fourth one."

"Did I say anything?"

"I could hear you thinking."

"You have good ears."

She frowned, looked at the cookie, and took another bite. Munched. After a moment, she swallowed. "Look, I don't do this every day."

"Good thing."

"I limit myself to one munch-out a month. It's—" He choked back a laugh, and she stopped. "What's so funny?"

"A munch-out?" Amusement highlighted the words.

"Well, what do you do when you're stressed?"

"Uh…"

"Play basketball or jog, I bet."

"Yeah. Unless it's really bad. Then I skydive."

"And you're making fun of me? At least what I'm doing won't get me killed." She slipped another cookie from the bag.

"So you say. All that sugar…"

"I limit myself to six at once. And only binge once a month. I keep track."

He nodded, grinning. "So what brought on the munch-fest?"

"Ryann."

He tilted his head.

She put the cookie back in the box. *Shouldn't talk and eat at the same time.* "I don't know how much you know, but Ryann was one of our staunchest teen leaders—after she went through a hard time of her own. When she went to college, she met this guy…"

"Not a Christian?"

"Yeah. I wish she'd gone to a Christian college or university and met someone whose faith was the same as hers."

"College is hard for many. They come up in the church, but all they've had is some pablum Christianity and fun times. Not enough to stand against the Enemy's tactics."

"Yeah. Well, this guy challenged all she'd been taught and did it with intelligence and kindness, too. I've met him. He's great except for that one thing."

"And that one thing has drawn her away from God?"

"And from her fiancé. She broke off the engagement."

A few minutes later, they stopped in front of the Life Center at the church and climbed from the SUV.

Reece glanced at her. "I'll unpack these. If you can find Josh, I need to know what's on the agenda tomorrow night."

"Jake is going to help with the youth. And China."

"Jake's the one in the Coast Guard?"

"Yes. He's married to China, Joshua's administrative assistant."

"She does a good job. So, will Ryann be here?"

"I have no idea. She hasn't been in church lately. She might not even know."

"Okay." He hefted a bag. "Can you find Josh for me and

71

ask him to come do some manual work for a change?"

Kati sent him a grin of her own and wound her way to the church office. She sighed. Pastor Alan should be here for this. She pulled the door open, heard talking from the back office, and dropped onto a chair.

Her mind rolled over the plans for the gathering. Her friend Lynn, along with China, had put their heads together to make it a success. They'd take care of the food she and Reece had bought. Miss Eleanor would head up the welcome committee. And Lynn's husband, Detective Rich Richards, would provide security. He hadn't been too pleased they'd asked the neighborhood on the north side. Too many robberies there, too many domestic violence calls. Kati stared at the wall. Families living with domestic violence needed help, too. And alcoholics. And families of alcoholics…

The voices—no voice—from the back room rose. Joshua's. And he was praying. Praying hard and loud and long.

Kati rose from the chair. Yes, the physical work was important, but the spiritual work more so. She crept toward the door and let herself out.

***

People filled the fellowship hall.

Kati counted the number of people helping out tonight. Besides Lynn and her detective husband, there was Jake and China, herself, Reece and Joshua, and twelve other people, plus some youth. They could have used more. Over a hundred people crowded into the Life Center. Who would have thought?

"It's the free food." Reece's voice sounded above her head.

She glanced up. "How did you know what I was thinking?"

"You're easy to read."

She shook her head. "Maybe it's because Josh prayed."

"Both." He nodded his head across the room. "So Mr. Coast Guard over there is having fun fending off the admirers."

"Jake and the rest of the crew were in the news again for saving a family whose boat was sinking. Sharks in the water. Real hero stuff."

"Ah. So that attracts the opposite sex. I need to sign on."

She rolled her eyes, and he laughed. They both glanced over the crowd.

Reece frowned. "What's with the guy in Josh's face?"

"I don't know. Looks like he's upset, though."

"Where's security?"

"Rich? He's here somewhere." Kati glanced over the crowd again. A lot of laughter and talk. No Rich. She turned to find Reece moving across the room, and she went after him.

The man talking to Josh leaned forward, well into his space. "I don't like the idea that my wife comes here without me. You can't trust people these days. Even pastors."

"You're more than welcome to come with her, Mr. Russo." Joshua's voice held a mellow, friendly tone.

The man scowled. "I told you I don't go to church. And I was Catholic—until all that stuff came out about the priests. Like I said, you can't trust people today." He looked Joshua up and down. "Nobody."

Josh nodded, smiled at the man. "I understand what you're saying. It's a hard world we live in. But—"

"No buts." The man's fists curled. "I don't want none of you people coming by my house anymore, and I don't want anyone talking to my wife. Is that clear?"

Kati felt the hair on the back of her neck rise. People around the man and Joshua stopped talking and looked their way.

Reece stepped into the man's line of vision. "We're just here to help people in the area, Mr...." He held out his hand.

The man's head shot around. He stepped back a foot, glanced down at Reece's hand but didn't shake it. "Who are you?"

"Just someone new to the area, glad to meet someone else

from the neighborhood."

The man's gaze swept him. "Do I know you?"

"We"—Reece nodded at Josh—"live down the road from you. We moved in about two months ago."

The man's gaze swept back and forth between them. "Maybe I saw the moving truck."

"Yeah, that would have been us."

"So, you two live together?"

Kati's brows rose at the man's tone. She stepped forward and took Reece's arm, leaned into him. "And it's been great having two such good-looking gentlemen in the area."

Josh smiled at her, then turned back to the man. "Mr. Russo, we'd be glad to have you at church, or please stop by our house sometime. We're neighbors. We'd love to get to know you."

Mr. Russo frowned at him. "Just remember what I said." He narrowed his eyes at Reece and strode off. No one said anything for a moment.

Josh lowered his head toward Kati's. "Good save. Thanks."

Reece grinned. "The woman's got sense. And a great eye for the finer things."

"What's that?" Her head came around. "What are you talking about?"

"About identifying the *gentlemen* in the neighborhood."

"Oh, you—"

"Ignore him, Kate, or he's going to keep teasing you forever."

"Humph!"

Joshua glanced toward the outside door as Mr. Russo exited. "Now there's a man we can add to our prayer list. He's one of the reasons we are doing what we're doing—reaching into the neighborhood."

Kati swept the room with a look. "We've had quite a few from the surrounding area here."

Joshua nodded and turned toward the buffet tables. "Is

there any food left? I'm starving."

Reece crossed his arms over his chest, tilted his head toward Kati. "That's a main complaint of his. Just so you'll know."

"As if it wasn't yours." Josh took Kati's arm and turned her toward the food tables. "Let's see what you two brought for us tonight."

Reece stepped beside them.

"I don't think much is left." Kati swept her arm forward, indicating the near-empty tables against the wall.

"Are there any cookies?" Joshua asked.

Reece began to laugh.

"What?" Josh asked.

Reece shook his head and walked off, chuckling.

"What's his problem?"

Katie frowned. "Nothing. He's just being...Reece, I guess. Yes, there are cookies left. In fact, I hid some."

"You did? You're a treasure. Don't tell anyone, but I'm a cookieholic."

Kati led the way to the kitchen, reached into the back of the cabinet, and pulled her box of cookies out. "Sugar cookies?"

He grinned. "I love them." He took three from the box. "Aren't you going to have any?"

"No, I...I've had my quota for the day."

He put a whole one in his mouth and tried to talk around it. "Oou've got displine."

"Yeah. About as much as a five-year-old."

He leaned back against the counter and popped a second one into his mouth, chewed, and swallowed. "Thanks for helping out tonight. I had no idea the response would be this good. It's gratifying."

Kati smiled. "Gratifying? Yeah, it is."

He tilted his head and chomped down a third cookie. "Reece is always telling me about my language. He says I need to speak like real people."

"Because you said *gratifying*? You don't need to talk like a fourth grader to be understood."

"Thank you. Both my parents are teachers, and my grandmother is a retired English professor. We read a lot of old books at home, watched old movies."

"Well, they did a good job of raising you."

He brushed his hands off. "They did teach me to say thanks when someone goes out of their way for me." His eyes twinkled. "Thanks. I bet that was your personal stash. Am I right?"

"You could say that."

"Let's return to the party. I don't want to be gone long."

"Kati!" China came through the door.

"Yeah?"

"Ryann's here. Just wanted you to know."

"Oh. I—"

Joshua pushed away from the counter. "Aha. Your friend. Come on."

The food was gone, and the crowd had thinned to about half, mostly church members chatting with whoever still remained. Ryann stood beside a tall, lanky man filling their cups from what remained of the drinks.

Josh clasped Kati's arm and slowed her progress. She sent him a question with her eyes.

He shook his head. "Do it casual. Be a friend first."

She nodded, but when she stepped next to Ryann, Kati couldn't help her wide smile. "Ryann, hey. I'm so glad you came. And that you brought Landon." She tried to keep her smile as she turned toward the man.

Josh put out his hand and shook Landon's. "I'm the assistant pastor someone tried to make a fuss over. Josh Corbin." He leaned between him and Ryann and whispered, "Just a ruse to get people into church. Let them see we're not such ogres after all." His mouth stretched wide, and he winked at Ryann. "Sorry you're late for the food. I think I just ate the last of the cookies."

Ryann slipped her arm through Landon's. "You mean you beat Kati to them?"

"What? Kate's a cookie eater?"

"Oh yeah. You are definitely new if you don't know of her addiction."

"Hey! Am I being attacked here?" Kati interjected.

Josh had let go of her arm as they neared the table, but now he squeezed it. "I'll keep your secret if you keep mine."

"Yeah." Ryann's face changed. "We all have secrets."

Landon pulled her closer. "Innocent ones like cookies. I wonder what kind of cookies?" He looked between Kati and Joshua.

"Any kind." Joshua's answer came quick. "So, Landon, have I seen you at church?"

The other man shook his head. "Sorry, Pastor. It's not for me. Been there. Done that. It didn't work."

"Really? We'll have to discuss that another time. I like a challenge."

"Not anytime soon. Ryann just wanted to stop by and wish you well. She used to attend regularly."

Kati tried to keep her face neutral. *Used to.* That was true. Because of him. Was the man just being obnoxious or throwing out another challenge? Her gaze went to Ryann. Had Ryann's mouth tightened?

Landon shot a look at Ryann, too, his face bland and amused. "About ready to leave, darling?"

Kati tried not to gag. *Lord, I'm sorry I'm so hard on the guy but...poor Ryann.*

***

Kati surveyed the Life Center's reception area. Early morning light filtered in through the windows lining one wall. Lynn had done a great job, as usual. And she and her team typically cleaned up afterward, but with Rich getting a call and having to leave earlier than planned, Kati just wanted to check everything.

The large decorative clock on the wall opposite said 7:14 AM, but after seeing Ryann last night, Kati had not slept well. A morning run to the church had made sense. No use wasting time tossing and turning at home.

Lynn had made sure her helpers cleaned the tables, but… Kati walked toward the door between the Life Center and the hall to the sanctuary. Someone had left the trash can right there. She reached for it and froze.

Words rumbled behind the door, and the next instant the door flew open, slammed into the trash can, and sent it spinning. Kati leapt for it before it spilled its contents all over the wood floor.

"Lord, we need you. We need your presence in our lives, in our services, in—" Joshua's voice dropped, stopped, and he stared at her in surprise.

She righted the trash can and grimaced. Why had she come so early? "I'm sorry. I didn't mean to interrupt your prayers."

"Oh, ah." He cleared his throat, looking sheepish himself. "I'm sorry, too. I…did I knock into that?" He indicated the trash can.

"No, well, I mean someone left it behind the door."

"And when I came storming through, I hit it? It's okay." His look changed to a grin. "I pray early because if I don't, the day gets ahead of me, and I run into situations that might have been avoided if I'd asked for God's help ahead of time."

Kati straightened and smiled, too. "Well, how do you know what to pray for if the day hasn't started? Oh yeah—"

"The Holy Spirit makes intercession through us for those things we don't know about. When I pray, I just let him lead." He took a deep breath. "And sorry, but I pray aloud and walk at the same time."

She shook her head, "Don't apologize. That's what we all want, a pastor that prays."

"Still getting used to being called pastor."

"What did you do before?"

"Anything *my* pastor would let me, but I love witnessing on the streets, in the homeless community, anywhere I can."

"Were you disappointed the biker gang didn't show last night?"

"Yes, in fact. Although I believe God had who he wanted here."

She nodded. "Ryann being one of them."

"Yes. I'm sorry I can't tell you more, but she needs a friend. Just be there for her."

"I plan on doing that." She tipped her head. "What would you have done if the gang had showed up?"

"Welcomed them. I hope you—the whole congregation— are getting that from my preaching, from the meetings we've had. I'm not a fighter, Kate. Not that way. My fighting is done in the spirit." He waved his arms back to the door he'd come through. "We don't fight against flesh and blood, but against principalities and powers, against spiritual wickedness in high places. Satan is our enemy; people aren't. It's something I decided a while ago. I'm not going to fight someone to protect myself. I'll let God do that, and if he doesn't, well, he doesn't."

She studied him. "You know, Joshua, you challenge me. I've played it safe for so long. I'm always worried that someone will take offense or be offended if I say something about my faith or about Jesus. But nowadays, I just want the passion back, you know?"

His smile changed his face. "Return to our first love, the Bible says. That's what we all need to do."

"So what do you think of me kickboxing? I mean, I do it to keep in shape but also for self-protection."

His brows came together. "My convictions are not yours. Yours have to come from God. Men and women go to war every day. Many feel led by God to do what they are doing. We do not all walk the same path."

Kati nodded. "You and Reece are so different. What's the story between you?"

He paused before leaning forward. "Reece saved my life."

Surprise shot through her. "He did?"

"It's a short story, but let's get some breakfast while I tell you. I'm starved."

They drove in his Jeep Cherokee to Chick-fil-A. Kati scooted into the booth across the table from him. The smells of chicken and coffee and warm bread encircled them.

She sat back, glad she'd be able to hear more about him and Reece. Joshua ordered two chicken biscuits, a large coffee, and a fruit cup. She'd ordered chicken nuggets and coffee. He talked about church things until the food was finished. After he scarfed down the two biscuits, he sat back and beamed.

"Thanks for giving me time to eat something."

Kati laughed. "You really were hungry."

"I get like this sometimes. I can't go on without food or sleep."

"Is that because you go so long without one or the other?"

"Good guess. Sometimes I just forget to eat or sleep." His head bent, then he lifted it. "There's so much to do. Jesus' ministry was only three years, and sometimes I feel like mine will be short, too. I mean, I feel I need to run. Time is short."

Kati leaned forward. "I know the feeling. I see the vastness of the call he has put on each of us—as citizens of heaven called to bring others with us. *Compel* them to come in, he says." She felt the awesome revelation, as she had at times before. "*Compel them.* He wants them, us, so much."

A smile spread again across Joshua's face. "Yes. We see it alike, but Reece says I could run them off with my coercion, that I forget about grace, and that God is bigger than my mess-ups and theirs."

Kati lifted her last chicken nugget. "He's got you there."

"Uh-huh." He stopped, hesitated. "Thank you for listening, for your encouragement." His gaze held hers for a moment before he straightened and cleared his throat. "But you wanted to know more about Reece and me and our friendship?"

"Yes."

"Well, what I said was true. Reece saved my life. I was trying to witness to some gangs in the city. I'd been on the streets every day for about a week, and a couple of guys took offense. Next thing I knew, I was on the ground, being beaten to a pulp. Kicked." He gave a half smile at her gasp. "Nice bruises, no broken bones. This guy appears out of nowhere and starts yelling. I couldn't see anything, bloody nose and all. The best I remember, there was some type of altercation. Next, I'm in an ambulance headed to the hospital, and that guy—Reece— follows the ambulance to the hospital. He's been around ever since. Sometimes I think Reece just hangs with me to make sure I don't get into trouble again." He stopped and stared down at his fruit cup. "But more than that, he keeps me balanced. And I need it. As I said before, a friend that sticks closer than a brother."

"Like Jesus said, and like Jonathan and David."

"Yes. I've heard that before. Only who's the Jonathan and who's the David?"

"Does it matter?"

Joshua picked up his coffee. "It does to Reece."

"Why?"

"Because as much as he talks about grace, he hasn't accepted it fully for himself. I can't get him to believe that just because he is who he is and I am who I am, that does not make me better than him or more spiritual. He can't see his worth sometimes. I want people to love God, to know how good he is, but if it wasn't for Reece, I'd probably cram that knowledge down their throats or at least talk them to death trying to get them to believe it."

"Is that a bad thing?"

His face stilled. "It is if you run them away from the very thing you want them to have."

81

***

Contentment filled Kati as they drove back to the church.

The goodness of God in the land of the living. The Scripture swirled inside her head. For so long she'd wanted to do something for God, to stir the zeal she used to have for him. And it was happening. Because of Joshua and his vision and what they were doing now. She liked talking with him. So many times she'd tried to talk with others about God and had felt shut down. Sometimes she was just too serious.

She sighed as they pulled up in front of the church, shaking herself from her thoughts, and scrambled from the car, then laughed as Joshua frowned at her.

He came to her side. "You're supposed to let me do that, woman."

"Open my door?"

"Yes." Amusement lit his eyes.

She shook her head. "And I just sit there while you get out and walk around? Silly."

"Rebel."

She laughed.

His smile was relaxed, tender. "You're easy to talk to, Kate."

She lifted her head. "Thank you for sharing all you did today."

His hand closed around hers. "You're welcome. Kati?"

His voice held a husky note she hadn't heard before. "Yes?"

His blue eyes searched hers. "I can't believe I've only been here a few weeks."

"I'm glad you're here."

"Are you? I feel like I'm in a whirlwind sometimes."

"You do?" That was a surprise. "Why?"

"Everything God is doing, how quickly it's coming together." He hesitated. "My feelings for you."

His feelings for her? Things stilled inside, became a blur. Her attraction to him was definite, but so was her attraction to Reece. That turmoil inside hadn't left, so she'd stayed away this last week. Joshua's warmth was palpable. She loved talking with him about God. Reece was intense, amused.

"I...I've felt that, too. The whirlwind."

He frowned. "Have you?"

"Along with the excitement of what's happening here, something whirling around, something uneasy."

He rubbed his hands up and down her arms. "That's the Enemy. Whenever God is doing something, Satan is too. Don't be afraid. Use your weapons. Your prayer and praise. The name of Jesus."

The words seemed almost rote; his eyes never left hers. In another moment, he pulled her to him and dropped his gaze to her mouth.

Kati didn't move. Joshua's eyes lifted, sought hers again, and then he lowered his head. His mouth moved soft and gentle over hers. She still couldn't move. His arms tightened, and the jerk of surprise inside evaporated. Warmth circled her. She gave in to the rising feelings and in to the kiss.

***

Reece rounded the corner of the building in time to see Josh pull her into his arms and drop his head for the kiss. He didn't know where it came from, but he had the sudden urge to grab his friend and land a fist against that smooth jaw. He hesitated for a second, taking in the picture of Kati in Josh's arms too long before he spun and walked the other way.

Of course she'd want Josh. She had a desire for God that matched Josh's to a T. Reece's mouth twisted. Josh was the one going somewhere, who knew what he wanted from life. For others, too. He was always thinking of others. Probably why Reece and Josh were good friends. They were opposites. Yeah. Reece had himself on his mind too much.

He took a deep breath, slowed his walk, realized how heavy his heart felt in his chest. Neither of them had known the girl that long. What was their problem? He crawled into his SUV. Slammed the door. Who knew Josh would make such a fast move? Was he even thinking straight? Nah. He was all hormones, and Reece was going to tell him so. Put him straight.

Put him straight, Reece? Don't you mean tell him to back off? That if anyone was going to put the moves on Miss Battle Maiden, it would be you, not him.

Great, Reece, just great. You sound like some fifteen-year-old kid. All hormones. Yeah. That was his own problem. Hormones.

Yeah, because the girl looked great kickboxing, looked great at church in that summer dress she'd worn. She laughed at his jokes and knew what he was thinking. She wore her heart on her sleeve, too, or maybe on her whole outfit. That was the problem…

Hormones. It was just hormones.

Chapter 6

Have I not commanded you? Be strong and courageous. Do
not be afraid; do not be discouraged, for the LORD your God
will be with you wherever you go.
(Joshua 1:9)

K ati leaned back against a table and considered the people
gathered together. Two weeks had passed since the security meeting, and excitement flitted from face to face around
the room. The congregation had embraced Joshua's idea of a
prayer walk, and after an hour of prayer this evening, the Life
Center buzzed with expectation.

An odd feeling, that acute anticipation, because she hadn't
been part of its growth. In fact, she'd stayed away from church,
except for Sunday services, until the prayer walk today. Not
being more closely involved had its price, but being here would
have caused other problems. Her glance went from Joshua to
Reece and back again. Her emotions over the last two weeks
hadn't solidified into anything tangible, and both men had kept
their distance this evening—which hurt in a way. And yet she
had kept her distance, too.

She threw a look heavenward. *We've got more to think*
about tonight than my feelings, right, Lord?

If Joshua had called or asked where she was, she would
have used work as an excuse. But he hadn't. In fact, their short

conversation after that kiss had indicated he might not, had let her know he wasn't quite ready for a relationship either. Her relief had surprised her.

Lynn and Rich approached. Lynn's model beauty balanced Rich's blue-eyed handsomeness. Kati smiled. Lynn had reached out to her when Kati first joined the church, along with Ryann and others.

"You okay, Kati?" Lynn's question followed a look of concern.

"Yeah. I'm fine. Looking forward to this."

"Me, too."

Rich's smile didn't quite make it to his eyes. It skipped past her and over the others in the room. "I counted thirty-six participants, which works well. We'll be walking three abreast on the right side of the road. Makes thirteen units. Hope no one is superstitious."

Kati almost tossed off his words, but she considered how his work with law enforcement and the fact that he headed up the security team would make this a different "walk" than the rest of the group anticipated.

Joshua stepped to the front of the room. "Everyone ready to head out?"

Murmurs of agreement and a few shouts and fist pumps met his question. The participants' enthusiasm made inroads into Kati, and as they exited the building, she grinned at Reece as he held the door for them. He winked and brought up the rear.

Joshua, Rich, and Lynn took the lead. Kati had heard Rich and Lynn arguing about Lynn's place in the walk. He didn't want her up front, but Lynn insisted they needed a woman so they didn't look so threatening.

"You"—she'd pointed at her husband—"are known by most people around here. They'll think this is a police program if they don't see someone looking approachable."

"Hey! I'm approachable." Joshua poked his head in between them. "But she's right, Rich. You should probably bring up the rear."

"Not happening."

"You're as obstinate as Reece."

At which they'd all grinned and dropped the subject.

Kati walked with China and Jake in the middle of the line, all walking abreast on one side of the road, allowing for traffic on the other.

She began to pray for the families living on both sides of the street, praying for health and blessing and salvation. She heard China's quiet prayers, and the quiet rumble coming from the rest of the marchers. Warmth and joy bubbled inside as they came to the end of the block and proceeded to the next.

Thank you, God, for allowing me to be part of this. Thank you for Joshua and Reece and for the heart of the people here. Many houses were in need of paint or lawn work. *Show us how we can help, Lord. Let our hearts be touched by the people here. Let them feel your love.*

A sheriff's cruiser was parked at one street corner, motor running. The deputy lifted a hand to Rich.

People appeared at windows, faces of all colors—black, brown, white. Some smiled. Most stared. A man came out of his house. His eyes narrowed as they passed. Cold ran up Kati's spine. *These are people you love, Lord. Help me love them, too.* She smiled and waved. His chin came up. Next to her, China also waved. He nodded then, hesitated, and went back into his house. A woman and two children came out of a house farther down the road. She held a young girl. The boy, probably eight, Kati guessed, came down the steps and stopped.

Kati waved and China did, too. The lady waved back, and some others in their group waved. One of the children darted into the street. His mother reached out to grab for him, but he slipped by her and ran to Kati.

"Whachalldoin?" He skipped beside her.

"We're doing a prayer walk. Praying for people in the neighborhood."

"How'd ya know what to pray for?"

"Well, some people have told us, and God tells us other things."

"God tells ya?"

"Well, he doesn't speak aloud. At least not to me, but he speaks in here." She tapped her chest. "Like I feel the need to pray for mothers right now. You know, mothers have it hard sometimes."

His face creased. "I know that. My mom does."

"Jameson!" His mom's voice reached them, and he grinned.

"I'm gonna get in trouble. But will you pray from my baby sister?"

Kati looked down. "Yes. Why?"

"She got some kind of cancer. It's serious."

Kati felt the tug on her heart. Oh, God, no… "I will. What's her name?"

"Jameson!"

He glanced back. "Her name's Shauna. Shauna Ayanna Williamson."

"Shauna Ayanna Williamson. I will, Jameson. I will pray for her."

He waved and ran home, leaving Kati's heart touched and pounding. *Lord, why didn't I bring something to write on? Please help me remember these names.*

Reece moved next to her. "You might have a friend."

"If I can remember his name and his sister's."

"What did he want?"

China looked over at Reece. "He asked her to pray for his sister. She has cancer. Wow. The Lord is working already."

Reece raised his head. "How about you, Coast Guard? You feeling this?"

Jake dipped his chin. "It's a good idea. I'm wanting to see

it play out."

Reece grinned. "Fair enough."

Jake glanced toward the front of the group and behind him. "It's a good turnout. It'll be good to see who stays and returns each month for the walk."

"The core group will. We'll see who they are." Reece moved ahead and passed the next couple of groups before stopping beside Joshua. Rich nodded at him and rolled back, passing them on the other side, heading to the last group.

Some people sat on their porches and waved as the prayer group passed. Kati waved at each one, praying under her breath for them as she walked past.

A woman and a teenage boy sat on one porch. The woman stood as they passed by and then grinned and waved at Kati.

She pointed to the boy beside her. "It's Josey and Martin. He's getting well."

The boy slapped at her and tried to shush her, but she looked down at him, said something, and pointed at Kati.

The boy looked up. His mouth inched upward, and he waved.

"Thank you for your prayers," Josey called after them.

"Who was that?" China asked.

"A patient. I'm so surprised she remembered me, that he remembered me. And so glad he is doing better."

"Ah. Again. The power of prayer."

"And a lot of antibiotics."

"Yes, but God could have put him in any hospital with any staff, and he obviously put him with a praying nurse."

Kati felt the truth of it sink home. "I never thought of it like that."

A motorcycle sounded behind them, and Kati stiffened. At the front of the group, Reece stepped aside and turned. The motorcycle edged closer, its sound a muffled roar. As it neared, Kati turned her head away, then stopped. She wouldn't glance at the man, but she wouldn't hide either. It passed by them at a moderate speed but slowed when it drew near Reece.

Someone touched her arm. "Señora? Señorita?"

Kati turned. "Yes?"

"You pray for my baby?"

"Sure, I would be glad to." She stopped walking, and when China stopped too, she waved her on. "Go ahead. I'll catch up."

The girl looked in her teens. Kati's heart tugged. "What's her name, or his?"

"Manuel."

"Manuel?" *Help me remember, Lord.*

"Sí. Sí. But he's sick. The doctors don't know what to do. He's been sick two weeks. They think he has flu, then said it's the food. It is not my food! I feed him good. I not hurt him. Please, you come. Pray for him."

"Come where?"

The girl pointed to a house across the street. "You come."

Kati glanced back as others in her prayer group walked past. Should she go? Maybe she should get someone to come with her.

"You come." The girl pulled on her arm. "You pray. Por favor."

Kati started across the street. "Okay, but—" She followed the girl, uneasiness filling her. *What should I do?* She bit her lip and stepped to the curb.

A hand gripped her shoulder. She jerked around.

Reece's lifted brow met her. "What's up?"

The girl stopped, too. Her eyes entreated Reece. "Mi bebé está enfermo. La muchaca va a venir a orar por él."

A line showed between his brows. "¿Dónde?"

She jerked her head in the direction of the house. "Mi casa."

He studied the house, glanced up and down the street before dropping his gaze to Kati. "You were going to ask someone about this, right?"

Kati put a hand on his arm. "Her baby's sick."

"So she said." His focus jumped between the two women. "Okay." He made a motion to someone in the prayer group, another to the girl, and they followed the woman into her house.

Sunlight filtered through the windows. Kati took in the older, well-used furniture but also that the house, although jumbled with toys, seemed clean. The woman urged them to a back bedroom.

A small boy lay on a single bed. A bone-white face highlighted dark-circled eyes. Kati's heart squeezed. The boy held up his arms to his mother. She scooted over, dropped onto the bed, and gathered him into her arms.

The girl talked to him in Spanish, and Kati waited. She could feel Reece close behind her, but she kept her concentration on the girl. After a minute, the girl waved them over.

Kati knelt by the bed. "Hey, Manuel. My name is Kati. And this is Reece." She glanced at him. "We're here to pray for you. Is that okay?"

His mother translated. The boy's eyes rose, wide and shaky.

"It doesn't hurt," Kati said.

Reece moved closer. "Te vas a sentir mejor después que la señorita Katy termine de orar por ti. Y entonces, tu mamá podría darte una Inca Kola."

The mother's eyes rounded, and Reece nodded toward the poster on the wall, showing Peru and a bottle of Inca Kola in the corner.

Kati looked from one to the other, then bowed her head and prayed. "Thank you, Lord, for Manuel and his mother and her belief that you can heal her son when the doctors don't know what is wrong with him. We know you do. Please heal whatever is causing these problems. Help his stomach to be well. Help him to eat without any trouble. And help his mother in all that she has to do. Provide for them. Thank you, Lord. Amen."

Kati bit her lip. It was a short prayer. Did the girl expect a long one? *Lord, it doesn't matter. It only matters that we ask and believe in you.* She took a deep breath, hugged Manuel and then his mom, and rose.

Reece stepped back. "¿Dónde está tu marido?"

"Afghanistan."

"A soldier?"

"Sí." Her eyes held sadness.

"A good man then?"

She smiled. "Sí. Un bien hombre."

Reece smiled, too, and backed from the room.

"What is your name?" Kati asked as they moved into the living room.

"Isabella."

"Well, Isabella, we would love to have you and Manuel come to the church when he is better. You know which church I mean?"

"Sí. We were there the other night. To welcome the pastor."

"Ah. I didn't see you. If you come again, please come say hello. I would love to get to know you and Manuel more."

Isabella nodded, but her eyes jumped to Reece as he dropped some money on her table.

Reece caught her look. "For Manuel. And Inca Kola."

Delight filled the girl's eyes. Kati almost laughed. Warmth wound itself around her inside. What a beautiful gesture. She glanced at Reece, but he only indicated the door.

"God bless you, Isabella. Come see us."

The street was empty. Kati glanced back and forth. "Where is everyone?"

He took her arm and drew her off the porch. "Around the corner already. You know, you cannot just walk off like that. You don't go into houses alone. Not if you don't know someone. If I hadn't glanced back and sized up the situation—"

"But she was so, so…pitiful. I was just going to be gone a minute. And I…"

"And you see how fast everyone is gone. Kati—"

"I get it. I wasn't sure, but how could I say no?"

"Just no." His voice was flat. "Or get someone to go with you. I don't mean China or Lynn. I mean someone on the security team. You don't—"

"Okay. Okay. Don't ruin the moment. Wasn't it great being able to pray for them? To be asked?"

His look raked the sky. "Yes, it was."

"Reece, you don't understand. I…"

"What?"

"This is my first time of really stepping out of myself, of doing something for someone else. I mean, something that is not safe and…and within my comfort zone. Oh, I witness at work some. It's easy there because people are hurt. They listen. But really, I'm such a minion when it comes to witnessing or anything like that. I've tried at the gym, too, but it's hard."

"A minion?"

"Not the cute ones. The nothing ones. You called me a warrior, but I'm not. Oh, I pray. I go to church. I do talk about Jesus—but only to those that don't slap me down right away. I…I'm ashamed of my fear. That's really why I took kickboxing. I thought if I could do that, if I could fight, I could stand up for Christ."

He had stopped with his head to the side, listening.

Kati dropped hers. "You…you're a warrior, not me."

"I wonder if you see yourself? Just because you're not on the streets witnessing does not mean you're not a witness, Kati. You help people. You're concerned for others. Your heart shows the Lord. You even wanted to help Terry get some cred back, as ridiculous as that sounds. Why? Because you felt for him—even if he acted like a jerk. And you're in my face when you don't like something. Oh yes, you're a warrior all right. And why do you put down prayer? Is what we're doing here, what you just did for Manuel, wasted? Do you have faith in it?"

"Of course I have faith in it, but—"

"But what? Get rid of your *buts*. Stop putting yourself down. The same God in me is in you. Your prayers move mountains. Your prayers put the devil to flight. The effective, fervent prayer of a righteous man avails much. And no, you don't have your own righteousness, but you have his. You are in him." He scowled at her. "Don't go saying you only pray, Warrior. Your prayers are weapons. Use them."

Surprise jolted through her, but she couldn't say anything. She was too humbled. Reece thought those things about her? God let him say those things? About her?

He grabbed her by the arm again and marched her down the street. How many bruises would she have from this man? At the corner, Rich waited.

But I'm nothing, Lord.

You're my daughter, and I love you.

The words came so quick that she jerked her head up. Reece and Rich were talking over her head. Reece still held her arm, but gently now, leading her.

Kati looked back and forth between them, then settled on Reece. "What did you ask her at the end?"

"What?"

Both men looked baffled.

"At the end. You put some money on the table, and you asked her something."

Reece's glare could vie with anyone's. Evidently mentioning that he'd left money on the table was not a good move.

"I asked about her husband."

"How did you know she was married?" His eye roll caused her to shake her head. "Well?"

"She had a ring."

Rich tried to cover his laugh but didn't succeed.

"All right. All right. So her husband's in Afghanistan, and

she's here on her own. I wonder where her family is."

"Well, señorita, you can ask her next time you see her."

"And that's another thing. Why are you so fluent in Spanish?"

"Joshua and I both took a course." He gave Rich a wry smile. "The man made me. He said we would need it. Of course, we did. We do."

***

Joshua parked in back of the church and walked to the office. On most weeks, he loved early Sunday mornings. The prayer walk had gone well. He opened the door to his office and went to stand before the window. The first rays of morning peeked behind the buildings—gray and silver and pink. It would be a beautiful day in Florida—hot and humid, yes, but a day God created nonetheless.

He ran a hand through his hair. His sermon had not come together yesterday, nor last night. Now he had just a few hours for God to give him what He wanted the congregation to hear. A swarm of bees seemed to surround him.

Not what I want. What you want, Lord.

Which was the best place to start. On his knees. He knelt down, desperate to stop the confusion in his head, to see clearly, as he had last week. Well, last week until he'd kissed Kati. What crazy thing had stripped away his mind and his self-control? She was lovely and strong and unique, yes. More than that, she was easygoing and agreeable, especially after the ping-pong games he and China played each day. China meant well, and she looked the avant-garde part—as if doing things differently would be her idea, not his. But she challenged every new thing he introduced. He'd been on his knees often for that very reason.

Am I doing what you want, Lord, and if so, why so much resistance? Satan, of course, was the enemy, not China. And

95

certainly not Kati. But why had he stayed away from her this last week or so, not called her?

He closed his eyes, began praying. His mind still spun. After the kiss, while still holding her, he'd had to tell her the truth.

"I'm sorry, Kate. I shouldn't have kissed you. Not that I didn't want to. I just don't know where I'm going yet. Here, at New Life Church, I mean. Things are still coming together, and I feel—what is the Scripture?—pressed on every side? I don't want to drag you into something that I'm not sure about myself." He'd moved to look at her. Her expression mirrored the confusion in his own heart. He held her against him, liking the feel of her in his arms, but soon she pulled away and insisted on going home.

"We both need to think through our feelings and pray about this." Her voice had been hesitant and low, and he started to pull her back but stopped himself.

What he'd said, what she'd said—that made sense. Just leave it for now.

That brought a measure of relief. He'd had the prayer walk to think about, and now Reece. Reece was his mainstay, his bastion of support, had been for the last three years. But this week… What was going on with him? They still joked and ribbed each other, but something was wrong. Josh's "You okay, bro?" had been met with differing levels of macho irritability.

"Why wouldn't I be okay?" Reece had asked. "Living in and planning for a walk in the worst neighborhood in town?"

"If I thought you couldn't handle that, we wouldn't be here. Besides that, man, what's up?"

But Reece had shut him out. Again.

Joshua rose from his knees, forked a hand through his hair, and walked from his office to the sanctuary. The Enemy was having a field day with him—and those he cared about. He opened the doors and stared inside the darkened building.

"Well, I'm not having it, you hear?" He raised his voice. "Not having it. Reece and Kati and these people belong to God. I'm putting you on notice. You, the Enemy of our souls. God is greater. In case you didn't know it, but you do. Back off!"

He strode down the aisle, lifting his words to God. "Thank you, Lord, for our safety, for your protection, and for whatever you have planned for us today. If I don't have a sermon, it's because you know I don't need one. Greater are you in us than he that is in world!" He marched past the platform and up the other aisle, and he began to sing.

The confusion swirling in his head, the swarm of bees, lessened. He'd be here praying and singing when the congregation came if that was what it took, but he was not giving in to doubts and uncertainty. God knew exactly what was going on and what was coming, and Joshua had already put his trust in Him.

***

He'd have to tell Manny, the worship leader, how much he appreciated him. The music, the songs and lyrics, filled him. God's presence seemed thick in the church. Joshua wanted to keep on worshipping, but something was stirring in his spirit. He studied the congregation and savored their expressions. Hearts open to God.

This, Lord, this is how it should be.

He hated to break the feeling in the sanctuary or stop the music, but he was stepping forward and doing it anyway. For some reason. He forced himself to speak. "Sit down, please. Sit down."

Good thing he had a microphone. His voice sounded rough and low even to himself. Most of the people had surprised looks on their faces. They weren't used to the worship time being cut short. Neither was he.

The congregation began to sit. Low murmuring and whis-

97

pering followed. The shuffling of papers added to it. He waited.

What is it, Lord?

Someone pushed open the back doors. Joshua stared as three men came in. One had his arm around Pedro Gonzalez's neck and a gun to his head. The other man—familiar—stood close behind them, holding the door. Four others slipped in and fanned out, two on either side, each with a weapon. Two had rifles Josh immediately identified as semiautomatics.

Shock jolted him. His head jerked in Reece's direction. Joshua's mouth opened, but nothing came out.

Reece soared to his feet, his eyes on the back door. "Everyone down!"

Even as Reece uttered the command, he pulled the gun from his underarm holster. Four other security members leapt to their feet, guns drawn and pointed at the intruders.

"Get down!" Joshua's voice echoed through the sanctuary.

Screams and movement followed.

"Pedro!" Maria's voice rang out.

"Hold your fire! Hold your fire!" Reece's words carried authority. "Maria, sit down!"

The woman hesitated, wide eyes darting between Pedro and Reece. Then she dropped to her seat. She bent her head. Her prayers sprayed across the sanctuary.

Joshua's heart slammed against his chest. He stared at the men fanned out across the back of the sanctuary.

God, help us!

The leader stepped forward, shoving Pedro in front of him. "Be quiet, woman. No one is to shoot, as the man said." The leader's gaze jumped to Reece, then skipped to the rest of the security team and halted on Rich. "I am here to talk. Only. If no one fires, neither will we. No 911 calls. Make sure you understand you have the safety of your people in *your* hands."

Joshua hadn't thought about having too many guns or too many people with them. A vision of wounded and dying people flashed across this mind. "No one fires. No. One. Fires. Let this man speak and get out of here without incident. Do I make myself clear? No heroics. No 911 calls. We will listen to what he has to say." His gaze went from Reece to the others.

Rich nodded. "You all heard Joshua. Do as he says." He focused on the leader. "What about Pedro?"

"We use him to get out and release him when we're away."

Joshua hesitated, then stepped from behind the bulletproof pulpit. "All right. You heard him. Let's make sure Pedro and everyone else is safe. Stay down. He says he's here to talk. Let him."

"Joshua." Reece's voice echoed in the quiet.

Joshua glanced down, and Reece jerked his head back toward the pulpit. Joshua sent him a frown. He wanted to ease the tension in the room, and if that meant moving from behind the bulletproof pulpit, he would. He focused again on the other man. "Can I know whom I'm talking to?"

The man's brows came together. He shot a look at Rich.

Rich spoke up. "Luis Ramirez, if our information is correct."

The man's glare hit Joshua in the gut. Whoa. The man didn't like Rich, or maybe just the police. He cleared his throat. "Luis Ramirez?"

Kati raised her head from behind a pew and turned in the man's direction.

Luis' glower jumped to her. His face changed. A smile flitted across it. "Well, señorita, we meet again."

"Kati, get down." Joshua's voice sounded harsh even to himself. He shifted his focus back to the man. "You have something to say?"

The man nodded. "Last night you and many of your people walked through our neighborhood. *We let you.* We heard you were coming. We watched to find out what you were doing. Many of you prayed, many smiled and said hello to those that came out of their houses. But one or two"—his eyes went to

Rich—"one or two asked the neighbors about us. Now, I'm trying to decide what to do about this." His arm moved under Pedro's chin. The gun moved, too.

Joshua's body tensed. His eyes met Pedro's. Saw the fear there. What had Rich done? "We were doing a prayer walk. Just walking through the neighborhood, praying for the people and their welfare. If anyone approached us, we stopped and talked and prayed for them if they wanted. We invited them to church, but no one should have asked about you or the gang." He scowled at Rich.

Rich grimaced and looked embarrassed.

"We do not mind if you do this prayer walk. In fact, we will make sure no one causes a problem—*if* you *only* do this and pray. Do not try to fool us. We will know if you use this for some type of police investigation. If that is your plan, you will find your time in the neighborhood to be muy peligroso."

Very dangerous.

Chapter 7

Finally, my brethren, be strong in the Lord and in the power of His might. Put on the whole armor of God, that you may be able to stand against the wiles of the devil. For we do not wrestle against flesh and blood, but against principalities, against powers, against the rulers of the darkness of this age, against spiritual hosts of wickedness in the heavenly places.
(Ephesians 6:10–12 KJV)

Joshua took another step forward. Reece shook his head, his face tight, and Joshua ignored him.

"I will make sure that incident doesn't happen again, Luis. You have my word. I appreciate—maybe not the way you've come in here today; I'm sure Pedro is not thrilled having a gun at his head—but I appreciate that you wanted to talk and nothing more."

Luis nodded. "Good. I am glad to hear that. You, señor, I trust." His glance roved the sanctuary, resting on Rich, then moving to Reece. His eyes narrowed. "I will also promise you safety in your house in the neighborhood if you keep your promise." He made a movement with his head, and the four soldiers on either side of him slipped out the back doors. He said something to the young man standing behind him, and he, too, disappeared.

Sirens sounded suddenly. Luis jerked around, then looked back at Joshua.

What had happened? Had someone texted to 911?

"Go, Luis. I will talk with them, hold them back until you let Pedro go and have time to get away. Go."

"Let's hope you do." The man backed out of the door.

"Nobody move." Joshua put steel in his voice. "Someone put Pedro's life in danger by calling the police. No one move. Reece and Rich, holster your guns, then follow them through the door slowly. Go out there and stop those deputies. These men came in peace, and we will honor that."

A low rumbling started among the congregation. People had risen, along with their voices. He had to focus; he had to hold them here. Luis needed time to get away. Pedro's safety was paramount. Some would agree with what he'd done. Some wouldn't, but he would deal with that later. Right now, with the threat gone, they would gain courage quickly.

"Okay, everyone, we're going to thank God for keeping us safe today, and ask for Pedro's safe return, too. Please pray with me." He took a breath. "Thank you, Father, for your protection..."

Across the sanctuary, voices rose. He heard Kati's and others he could identify. His heart swelled with thanksgiving. But if anything happened to Pedro, he would never forgive himself.

In the midst of the prayer, Reece came back in with Pedro. Joshua jumped from the platform and raced up the aisle. Others noticed, and the prayers died.

Joshua threw his arms around the man, squeezed him in a grizzly hug. "Pedro, gracias a Dios que estás salvo. Praise God you're safe!"

"Sí, sí, hermano. Gracias a Dios!"

Maria rushed forward. "Pedro! Gracias a Dios! Gracias a Dios!"

Joshua stepped back, grinned, then circled around them and headed out the door. He looked into flashing lights and the eyes of a deputy standing next to Rich. Other cars, lights pulsing red and blue, pulled into the parking lot.

"I'm the assistant pastor, and I don't know who called you,

but we are fine here."

***

Joshua swiped a hand through his hair. The day after the gang members' visit had brought some interesting people to his office. It would be easier keeping rein on a bunch of toddlers in the Macy Day's Parade than a congregation confronted with gang members holding rifles and guns. And easier handling the gang members than Miss Eleanor.

The octogenarian leaned forward now, her face surrounded by white hair and set in firm lines, her blue eyes alive and boring into his. "Saying that these hooligans—who had a gun to Pedro's head—came in peace was fantastic nonsense." She waved a hand for quiet as he started to speak. "No, young man, you listen to me. I've been retired longer than you've been alive. I've seen every sort of revival you can think of. And I've done my share of street ministry and mission work, too."

He'd wondered from where the opposition would come, but he hadn't seen the Enemy's attack on Miss Eleanor. So far, she'd been a starch supporter, an intercessor, a warrior. The others who had come today, three men and one woman, would create a vacuum when they left. He had no doubt from their tone and words that they would, but it was not unexpected. Others would slip away without confronting him. He'd known the day God had put this on his heart that some would leave. He couldn't blame them. They had families, young children or teens that they wanted to keep safe. And God hadn't called everyone to the same ministry. But Miss Eleanor…

"I need you."

She sat back. "What?"

"Miss Eleanor, besides Pastor Alan, you are the backbone of this church. Everyone respects you. I respect you. The congregation feels that if anyone could walk on water besides Jesus—and Peter—that it would be you. I need you."

She scrutinized him. He tried not to feel like a ten-year-old boy under that scrutiny, and he surrendered the situation to God.

Her mouth formed a thin line. "I'm not really interested in whether you need me or not. I'm interested in whether what you're doing is of God or not."

The restraint on his spirit was strong. *Tread lightly, carefully. Let there be no division.* "Miss Eleanor, until Sunday, you believed God was directing me, directing what we're doing here. If you harbored any doubts, I was unaware of them."

"Until Sunday, yes."

"I do not want to sound impertinent, but has God's heart toward these people changed?"

Her jaw tightened, and her cobalt eyes darkened. "You know God doesn't change. If he called you here, if he gave you the vision you've given us, then nothing has changed. The question, Joshua, is, did we all get carried away by your passion and not hear God after all?"

He met her look. "That is the question. Did God call me here? Did he give me the vision I've tried to share with the congregation?" He rose and moved from behind the desk to sit in the chair next to her. "It's something I questioned all night. Something I will question more. I've called Pastor Alan, as I said when you first entered. I expect his call this evening. A lot rests on his shoulders."

"A lot rests on yours."

He nodded. "Yes. Yes, it does. I can be bullheaded—at least Reece tells me that—but I want more than anything to serve God, to walk in obedience to Him. I don't want anyone to get hurt because I've been foolish or stubborn." He waited for her to say something, and when she didn't, he continued. "I did not feel any change in God's leading after seeking him last night."

She stood slowly, waved a hand to keep him seated, and studied him. "I will think and pray about what you've said. I

104

heard nothing last night either, but I assumed it was because in my mind's eyes, I kept seeing men with rifles and guns at the back of our church. You mean well, Joshua, but this...this situation needs more than that."

He tried the briefest of smiles. "That, Miss Eleanor, is an enormous understatement."

As Miss Eleanor exited, China stuck her head around the corner. "You have another visitor."

He walked around his desk and slumped into the chair, dropped his head a moment, then lifted it and forced a smile. "Okay. Send them in."

China nodded and slipped back out the door.

Just then, he saw God's blessings in China. She was efficient, knew the ins and outs of this office, and kept it running despite an assistant pastor who knew next to nothing about that. *Thank you, Father, that in the midst of all this, I have someone who knows what she's doing.*

He took a deep breath. *And thank you for protecting us yesterday. Thank you.*

The door opened. He looked up. Isabella slipped into the room, Manuel on her hip. She approached his desk shyly.

He sat up, lightness lifting the heaviness of a moment before. "Isabella, what are you doing here?"

"I...I wanted to come. You forgive me if I disturb you?"

"You're not disturbing me. Sit down. Is Manuel okay still?"

Her smile was wide. "Yes. Yes, he is. Ever since Señorita Kati and Señor Reece prayed for him. You knew that, yes?"

"Yes, I did. God healed him."

"Sí. Sí. I...I needed to come for another reason."

"Well, I'm glad you did. I've seen you in church, but don't get much chance to talk."

"I know. I have to leave. Mateo, he waits for me down the street. To take me home."

"Ah. Your husband is in Afghanistan, Reece said. Is Mateo

your brother? A friend?"

Her head dropped. "My brother."

"He doesn't like church?"

Her head jerked up, face flushing. "No. He hates church."

"I understand. It's nothing for you to be embarrassed about. We all have relatives who do not belong to God. We can pray for him."

The flush remained on her face, and her voice rose. "Señor Josh, it is more than that. I...I heard him on the phone. My brother, he is in a gang, and they want to hurt you. You must warn Señor Reece and Señorita Kati, too."

Ten minutes later, she'd left, and Joshua knew he had a few phone calls to make—the police, Rich Richards, Reece...and Kati. He bit his lip. Isabella had nothing specific, and it could have been just a tirade of her brother's. Maybe.

He put his head in his hands. Or the threat could be real even as the fire at the gym had been real. The police hadn't found out who was responsible for that, maybe never would. *You saved us yesterday, Father. I know that. I thank you. Obviously we're going to need your protection again.* He slipped to his knees. *I have no strength for what you're calling me to do, much less to ask others to do it. You know I'd give my life for Pedro, or for Reece or Kati or Miss Eleanor. Or any of the others. I think. As far as I can see inside me, I could do that. But if I had to watch one of them die...* A knife blade to his gut would be easier to take.

And what if you asked me to do it for someone like Luis Ramirez? Where would that come from? If you want me to stand in that pulpit again and encourage people to give their lives—in whatever fashion—you'll have to pour more into me. More love, more courage, more compassion, more strength. More...of yourself.

***

106

Kati waited at the door to the waterpark while Reece parked the van. He still grumbled. She couldn't help her laughter.

He'd grumbled all the way here. "I don't do kids. I don't do waterparks and screaming and telling kids not to run or they might get hurt. And staying overnight with twenty teenage boys…"

He'd let it trail off, but she knew what he meant. Staying overnight would mean no sleep and lots of stress. Which was why she'd rented her own cabin. She'd take the one or two troublemakers or anyone feeling lost, but she'd leave the rest of the girls to China and Cindy.

"Of course you do. Everybody does. At some time. Besides, you'll love it."

He'd shaken his head as he climbed onto the bus. Jake was driving, and Kati and China and another couple were along as chaperones, but they'd needed one more guy, and with no one else available, Josh had volunteered. Only Josh had received a call from the police…

She giggled as Reece marched up to the door. "You look like you could murder someone."

"Josh is on my list."

"Oh, come on, bear. You know you loved this as a child."

"Whoever said I was a child?"

She glanced up as they paid and passed through the gates. "Everyone is a child."

"Some have more luck with that than others."

Screaming and laughter and the sound of gushing water rose to their right. Kati wrinkled her nose at the ever-present smell of chlorine. Reece looked around and rolled his eyes. Kati touched his arm, concerned suddenly about his growing-up years, about which she knew nothing. Had he been able to be a child? Had he been abused? She raised her head, and his eyes slid sideways.

"Don't worry about it. I'll be all right. I can grab a kid from the deep end as well as the next person."

"Josh did say you knew how to swim."

"Yeah. Neighborhood pool and all that. My grandmother made me take lessons."

Three girls shoved by them and raced for the wave pool. Two boys did the same.

"Did she?"

"Yeah. She loved swimming, so she thought I would too."

"And you don't?"

He scowled. "Do you know how often you can swim in New York? Not much. Not like here."

She jumped aside as another group of teens raced by them. "Have you been swimming here? I mean, in the Gulf?"

"At the beach?"

"Yeah."

"I went one evening."

She slapped his arm. "You don't go swimming in the evening."

He looked down at his arm and back to her. "Why not?"

"Sharks. Crazy. Sharks feed at night."

He studied her a moment. "Truth?"

"Of course. Was that the only time?"

"How long do you think we've been here? Josh and I went twice when we first arrived. Had to make it to the beach. Then things got busy when we found the house and with the church."

Someone yelled their names. Kati shot her head around. China waved before she and a number of girls disappeared up the steps to a high flume.

"Come on. Let's do that monster ride. Most of the kids are on it."

Reece stared at the steps leading high up into the building. "I haven't done this since I was fourteen. They've changed some."

"You're not scared, are you?"

His eyes narrowed. "No."

She grinned. "Come on then. I can't do it alone. You have to weigh two hundred pounds or have a combined weight of two hundred pounds."

"Two hundred?"

"Yeah." She started climbing the stairs.

"Hey, Kati. You and Reece gonna ride?"

Kati glanced up and saw the girls from her Bible class staring down from the top of the stairs. "Yeah. We're coming. Well, if I can convince Reece."

The girls laughed. She heard Reece's growl close behind her and hurried up the steps, amusement rising again.

When their turn came, she climbed onto the tube, caught the handholds, and adjusted her legs to give him room to climb in. He averted his gaze and climbed onto the tube too.

She stared at him, aware of his averted gaze, and tried to put her legs in a way to hold her balance and that wouldn't seem…what? Provocative? *Don't cause your brother to stumble, Kati.* It was why she opted for more conservative swimsuits and clothing. Most of the time. Obviously the clothes she'd started wearing to the gym had caused some stumbling. She'd changed that, too. Even if it was for Reece. But she sure didn't want some of the other members there salivating over her. She shuddered and looked back at Reece.

Him with the wet T-shirt over the tattooed, muscled body. She dropped her eyes this time. As if you could be around Reece and not be aware of the physical. Yeah, like a wet T-shirt. What a change on that one. She laughed, and he looked at her finally.

"Sorry. I just thought of something."

The water gushed forth and pushed them away from the side. The tube spun. Reece fell back and caught himself.

"Hold on!" Kati yelled. Delight spurted through her.

Screams and laughter came from below, and they went shooting and spinning and water-sprayed down the tube. Her screams rose with the others. Minutes later they fell into the pool below and come up gurgling and smirking and laughing.

She hit the water with the side of her hand and sprayed him. "You pretended you never did this before. You're a pro."

He waded to her, looking down, eyes dancing. "Not a pro. I just held on."

"Come on," one of the girls yelled. "Let's do it again." She ran toward the stairs with the others.

"You game?"

"Me?" Kati gave an indignant face. "You mean, are you?"

He grabbed her arm, and they hurried after the others.

"Wait a minute." Kati skidded to a stop. A girl from the youth group stood to one side, by herself. "There's Susan. Let's grab her. She's all alone."

Reece's mouth hitched, and he turned in the girl's direction.

"Susan, come on with us." Kati grabbed her arm. The smell and the feel of sunscreen met her nose and her hand. Good girl. She'd listened to their advice.

When the girl pulled back and shook her head, Kati laughed. "Come on. You can do this. Reece and I will keep you safe."

"It's all right. I've done it before."

"Good. Come on then." Kati pulled her forward, and the girl surrendered. They ran up the steps after the others.

***

Dinnertime had arrived, and Kati slipped away from the others. She'd planned on some downtime on her own. The two women didn't need her in the big cabin to chaperone, but she was still sure one or two of the girls would come to her cabin tonight and beg to sleep there. She was also of aware of Reece's scrutiny as she escaped. He'd probably give her grief tomorrow for running out on them, especially after her own remarks to him.

110

The cabin was surrounded by trees, and a long path led back to the waterpark. She leaned back in the deck chair and let it ruffle her hair. An evening breeze helped dry the thin line of perspiration on her skin. She sighed. Her mind wandered back through the day, the girls, the pranks, the laughter. Reece. She'd seen another side of the man as he'd relaxed, joined in a prank or two on the other chaperones, and indeed had pulled a kid from the deep end.

A cardinal chirped and flitted through the trees nearby. The scent of pine permeated the air.

She smiled, thinking about the look on Reece's face when Jeffrey had not surfaced when he should have. His concern changed into a flying leap into the wave pool, and he dragged Jeffrey upward by his hair. Jeffrey's cough had cleared what little water he had swallowed, and both man and boy stared at each other and hugged. A couple minutes later, Jeffrey was back in the water, but at the shallow end.

"Kati!"

She heard the emphatic sound of her name before she made out Reece jogging the path to her cabin.

She stood. "Is something wrong?"

"The girls are on their way, Battle Maiden. You might want to get inside."

"What girls? What are you talking about?"

"I came to save you."

"From what?"

He took hold of her arm and pulled her along the deck. "The girls. I heard part of their conversation. You're alone here in this cabin, and that makes you a target." He pushed open the cabin door. "Inside."

"What?" She tried to free herself.

"Food fight. Coming to you. Unless you're into that. At the time, there were about eight of them." He shoved her inside.

"Food fight?"

"They're bringing it. You should have been at dinner. As I

111

said, prime target." He shut the door.

"But, but…" She closed her mouth and thought. "There's two of us."

"Oh, no. All this Play Station stuff is not me."

"Come on, Reece. We've got to defend ourselves."

"*Yourself.* I just came to warn you. Eight to one didn't seem fair. And they're bringing leftovers. Lots of leftovers."

"Hmm… Well, yeah, I have hardly any food here. Snack bars, stuff like that." Her eyes darted over the cabin. "I've got water."

He rolled his eyes. "Water fight? I can't believe you'd do this. Just stay inside, turn off the lights, and close the drapes." He made a move toward the light switch.

"Reese! You have to fight. You can't just hide."

"*I* have to fight?"

"Yes. You're on my side now. You're here. And they'll never let us live it down if we don't fight. Where have you been all your life?"

He stared down into her eyes. "Let's say my fighting had more reality to it."

"Come on. Let's fill up as many containers as possible." She glanced out the window. "You're sure they're coming?"

"Oh yeah. They were just looking for things to carry the stuff in."

She ran to the kitchen, yanked open cabinet doors, and began pulling plastic containers from them. "The trash can! Get the trash can and fill it up. Use the tub. Hurry."

He hesitated a minute, eyeing her.

"Come on! You said we don't have much time." She shoved the plastic trash can at him. "Fill it up. Just make sure you can throw the water at them."

He disappeared down the hallway. Kati stuck a bucket under the faucet and grabbed another container. He returned just as she finished filling hers.

A quick glance out the window drew a grimace. "Here they

come."

She laughed and hurriedly closed the kitchen blinds. "Just in time. Let's sneak out the back door."

"You're into this, aren't you?"

"Oh yeah. Come on."

Pounding sounded on the front door. "Kati. Hey, Kati, open up, will ya? We brought you some dinner." Laughter followed.

Kati rolled her eyes at him. "They think I'd fall for that?"

"You would have."

She sniffed. "Maybe."

"No maybe about it."

She shushed him. They stole out the back door and around the side of the cabin. The girls were gathered together on the front deck in front of the door. She motioned to Reece, and they crept forward.

One of the girls turned and gasped. "Hey!"

The others turned, and Kati ran forward and tossed the bucket of water at them. They screamed, and Kati turned to run back, almost knocking Reece down. Food came her way, and then Reece stepped up and heaved the trash can full of water the girls' way. More yelling followed, and she and Reece raced for the back door.

Reece pulled her back into the cabin and slammed the door. Laughter from the outside met their own. Something slopped against the door and slid down.

Kati doubled over, her sides hurting. "As much as it doesn't look like it, I think we won."

"Do you? This counts as a win?" He pulled her upright and pushed her against the door, grinning like Disney's Cheshire Cat.

"Oh, it does." She giggled. "I loved your garbage throw. Did you see them scatter?"

A wide smile lit his eyes. "I love your laugh."

"You do?"

"And I love how you want to help others—like Susan."

She blinked, sobered. His voice was rich with laughter still and yet somehow serious. Her back was against the door, and when he leaned forward, his weight pinned her against it. And then he turned his head, and his mouth was against hers, molding itself to hers. His tongue invaded her mouth. He wrapped his arms around her, their tightness and the intensity of his kiss leaving little room for breath.

From somewhere she heard the girls pounding on the door and yelling at them, but it made no difference.

"Kati." His mouth moved to her chin and then her neck, and she clung to him so she wouldn't fall. Every muscle melted. His mouth moved back up, covering hers, making it his again.

She had to pull away, had to stop before it got out of control. Nothing in her wanted to, but from somewhere inside the strength came. She pushed against his chest, murmured against his mouth. "Reece."

He drew back slowly, his mouth leaving hers, his eyes meeting hers. And then they closed. His face went slack, and his arms loosened. "I'm sorry, Kati. I got lost for a moment. You in that bathing suit all day, laughing like you do…" His eyes searched hers as if he sought understanding, and then he stepped away. His arms dropped to his sides.

She touched his arm. It had felt so good—the kiss, his arms around her. She shook her head, leaned into him again. "It's okay."

"No. No, I'm sorry." He straightened, moved his shoulders back. His face tightened. "You and Josh…"

"Me and Josh? What are you talking about?"

"He hasn't said anything, but…I saw you."

"What? You saw what?"

He heaved a sigh and stepped farther away. "This never should have happened. I need to go."

"Why?" Confusion ricocheted through her. She dropped her gaze to his mouth. He was sorry about the kiss? An ache began inside her.

Light glinted through his face, then it left, and his face settled into a mask. "You and Josh. I won't get in the middle of that. I can't."

She took a step forward. "Reece, you're not in the middle of anything. What are you talking about?"

"I saw him kiss you."

Oh, Lord, help me. "He did kiss me, but he hasn't…hasn't followed that up in any way."

Reece hesitated, seemed to wait, but then shook his head. "Of course he hasn't. It's too soon. He doesn't know how all this—the gang, your friend Ryann—all that will play out. He'll keep you at a distance until he does."

"What? Keep me at a distance? Is that what he's doing? What if I don't want to be at a distance? And what if…" She stopped, searching his face. He was sorry about the kiss? She swallowed. *What if I want* you, *Reece, not Joshua?* She'd almost said it aloud. But was it true?

Between Reece and Joshua… Her mind swirled every time she thought about it. In fact, she'd tried not to think about it. She'd only tried to stay away from both—and done a terrible job of that. Obviously.

She dropped her head, then jerked it back up. "What does Ryann have to do with anything? Is Josh interested in Ryann, too?"

Reece's eyebrows jumped. "No. No, Ryann has nothing to do with this." He looked like a little boy suddenly, confused, uncertain.

"Yeah, sure."

He took her arms. "No, Kati. Josh is not like that. Ryann has nothing to do with this."

"Then why did you mention her?"

"Look, this is going from bad to worse. I need to leave." He moved her aside.

"What is going on? I don't understand any of this. Why are

you running off?"

He looked hunted, and he grabbed the doorknob.

She put her hand out. "Don't leave. I—"

"I have to." He wrenched the door open and yanked it closed behind him.

Kati didn't move.

What had just happened?

***

Reece's chest felt heavy, and he searched the starry sky as if he'd find the answer there. The sound of the waves from the Gulf waters eased some of the hurt, the guilt. Its far-reaching endlessness reminded him of God. As he'd told Kati, he'd come here a few times since they'd arrived from New York, and the constant rush of the waves, the sheer vastness of the waters, awed him.

He'd told Jake something had come up and he needed to leave. He couldn't face Kati again, not this soon. He needed to get himself in hand. Put some space and time between them. Jake had assured him they'd be okay.

He couldn't believe he'd let himself get carried away like that. Kati was beautiful and bright, and her laughter filled him with a sense of happiness and hope. Hope that he could be better, that he might be what she'd want, that… He stared into the night before dropping his head. How could he do that to Josh? He hadn't made a play for her. It had just happened. The kiss, her in his arms, the strength of his desire for her.

Josh had told him Christian girls were different from those he'd been with before. Many believed that sex was between a husband and wife only. That idea had taken getting his head around. Along with Josh pointing out Scripture that backed that up.

Josh told him that even if a girl did have sex with him, she'd think he'd marry her—which really scared him. He supposed that was how so many Old Testament prophets ended up with too many wives. Not going to happen with him. In the three years since his salvation, he hadn't even kissed a girl. Until today.

He'd felt Kati's response, the way her body melded to his. But marriage…that would be what she wanted. And should be wanting with someone like Josh. Not him. Not the guy from the streets who didn't know how to act. Or talk. He could communicate with the homeless, with gang members, but he didn't have the words like Josh did to talk with others.

His high school diploma came from a GED that Joshua had forced him to study for and get. It wasn't that Reece wasn't smart; he just wasn't book learned. Books scared him. Except for the Bible. For some reason, he could read that and understand things far beyond his education.

Waves crashed at his feet, and he stepped back, inhaled the salty air, and fought his throat. How was it that the man he loved more than a brother could cause this wash of darkness through him?

No, it wasn't Joshua. It was him, Reece, and his desire for Kati. And not just physically. But something more. The hope around his heart scared him. She'd responded to his kiss. She'd acted as if…

Heaviness hit like a wave, knocking him back. It was just like his dad always told him, Reece was good for nothing. Even when Reece had last visited him in prison, his dad had said the same thing. "You're good for nothing." His father wasn't impressed by Reece's faith or the new direction his life had taken. *Good for nothing.* He'd thrown it at Reece again as he'd left.

He stepped quietly into the dark house, shut the door without a sound. Or tried to. Someone stirred on the couch. He spun around, his hand going to the gun beneath his jacket.

"You're back." Josh's voice.

Reece dropped his hand and stretched his neck. "Why don't

you have the light on? I almost shot you."

He heard movement, and the next instant the end table light went on. Joshua sat up, yawned, blinked, then stared at him. "Where have you been?"

"What? Are you my mother?" He tried to keep a light tone.

"Kati texted. She asked if you were home yet, asked if you were okay. I thought I'd see you soon after her text, thought maybe we'd catch dinner." His eyes bored into Reece.

Reece turned and walked to the kitchen. Dinner might have been a good idea. He opened the refrigerator.

"So, bro, are you okay? What's up?"

Reece dug around until he found the ziplock bag of pizza leftovers. "Nothing. You want me to report in or something?"

"Yeah, I'm your mother. Report in." Joshua stood. "What's going on?"

"I scored some crack. Okay?" He slapped the pizza on a paper plate and shoved them into the microwave.

"Yeah, I believe that, just like I believe nothing is going on."

Reece whirled. "I told you I don't do teenagers. I didn't want to spend the day in the kiddie pool. You forced me. Just leave it at that. I'll get over it." He turned, grabbed a Coke from the refrigerator, and slugged it down.

Joshua's look pierced him. "I'm sorry. I told you I'd planned on going. The Sheriff's Office thought their demand on my time was more important."

"Yeah. You said."

"Reece, you had Kati and other adults. I don't believe whatever is going on has to do with this."

"Yeah. I had Kati."

"What's that supposed to mean?"

"That you should have been there, bro. *You*. Not me. She looked good in that bathing suit. You would have appreciated it."

Josh frowned. "I thought we agreed that Kati was off limits, that we had too much on our plates."

Reece grabbed the pizza from the microwave and rotated toward him. "Yeah? Then why were you kissing her, man? Looked pretty 'within limits' to me."

"Is that what this is about? Okay. I kissed her and have regretted it since. I like her. More than that if I let myself." He ran a hand through his hair. "I had to back out of that one, and it was hard."

"Back out? What do you mean back out? You playing with her?"

"I don't play. You know that. Or should." He laughed. "Neither of us has had a relationship since we've known each other. What do we know? Look, are you thinking I made a move after I said we needed to stay clear of the girl? Well, if so, you're right. Not planned, but…there. She's attractive, and more than that, she sees my vision. She's easy to talk to, to work with, to—"

"Yeah, yeah. I get it." He stood at counter, feeling Josh's eyes on him, and forced the food down. "What?"

"I make mistakes, Reece. I'm not Mr. Perfect. I made a mistake with Kati. It won't happen again. At least, not anytime soon. The cops want our cooperation. I can't have that and do everything else. You know what I can do and what I won't do. It will be a tightrope. We need you. I need you."

Reece dumped the leftover pizza in the trash. "Well, get over it. I told you I won't be here forever. Maybe I've overstayed my welcome already."

"No, you haven't."

Reece twisted his head back and forth, stretching the muscles. "Look. I messed up, too. Big time."

"How? What did you do?"

"I mentioned Ryann to Kati."

"You mentioned Ryann? How would that even come up?"

"Long story. One I'm not going in to."

Joshua frowned, shifted back and forth. "You mentioned

her? But with what reference?"

"Nothing. Nothing that Kati guessed at." Reece lowered his head. Bed sounded good right now. Anything to get free of this interrogation.

"You want to know what I think?"

Reece blew out an exasperated breath. "No, bro. For once, I don't."

"I think someone, something, has been coming down on you. That you've lost that knowledge of grace you're always talking about. Who's been in your face? Let me know. I need a word with them."

"No one. You're way off base."

"Way off base, am I? Then there is something."

"Drop it, man. You're going to get a face full of fist."

Joshua lifted his chin. "Here's a target."

Reece shoved past him. "Don't give me your stuff. I've seen you on the street."

"And I've seen you. I've seen your heart. Praying with gang members, hugging them…crying."

"Shut up."

"What's gotten into you tonight? You haven't been like this for ages."

"You're into me, man. You are. Mr. Perfect. All right, you made one mistake. Well, my life's a mistake."

Joshua grabbed his arm, and Reece rounded on him, fist curled. Josh didn't flinch. "Jesus doesn't make mistakes. *You* are no mistake. In fact, I think you're one of God's better ideas. You. Reece Jernigan. And God didn't set you free of your addictions and self-loathing to have you sink back into them. God was and still is in pursuit of you, and He's not letting go. I'm not letting go. Whatever is going on inside of you, it's a lie. From the pit. You know it. I know it."

Reece froze. Was it a lie? *Good for nothing.* He hesitated. No. He wasn't good for Kati or Joshua or God. "Let go, Josh."

"You're the one that wants to be Mr. Perfect. Well, none of

us can do that. It's not in us. If it was us, it wouldn't be Him. We talked about this before. You're accepted because of His shed blood, and that blood has made you *faultless*. Shake this off, Reece. Believe what God has said, not what the Enemy is saying. God loves you."

Reece swallowed, peeled Josh's hand off his arm, and moved toward the doorway.

"Reece!"

His mind swirled. The darkness hovered. He shook his head and went out the door.

Chapter 8

*And do not be conformed to this world, but be transformed by
the renewing of your mind, that you may prove what is that
good and acceptable and perfect will of God.*
(Romans 12:2 NKJV)

W hat happened yesterday, Kati?"
      Her head came up from the boxes she'd been going
through. Josh had settled into his office now, but still he'd determined to go through the boxes of books others had left, before giving them to the local library and maybe from there to
the dump.

"Yesterday?"

"Yeah. At the waterpark. What happened with Reece?"

Dismay shot through her. She'd left the waterpark early this
morning to get back. When she'd stopped by the church, she'd
hoped to see Reese. Instead, she had found Joshua and hung
around, still hoping, but to no avail.

"With Reece?"

"Yeah." He ran a hand through his hair. The line of his
mouth looked hard. "I haven't seen him like that in…years."

Alarm pierced her. "What do you mean? Like what?"

"Wallowing almost. Down. I'm no good." He slammed a
book against his desk.

Kati jumped.

"He went out last night and didn't come back."

Dread cramped her heart. Late-afternoon sun came through

the office window. "You…think he's in trouble?"

Josh's eyes held a grief she hadn't seen before. "I hope not. He's had a few crashes since he gave his life to God. But you should have seen him—that warrior that fought for my life that day. I said I didn't remember because what I thought I saw at the time was Samson fighting the Philistines with the jawbone of an ass." He stopped, gave a half smile. "That would be *donkey* to you. What I actually saw was Reece with something in his hand, laying into five—five, Kati—guys, and then I remember nothing until the hospital. And since then I've seen him fight in prayer for others, with tears in his eyes for those lost to drugs and prostitution. He'd just come to God a few days before he saw me being beaten. He jumped in to help with no thought to himself. That's Reece. Others are more important."

Kati swallowed. "You…you and Reece used to minister on the streets?"

"Yes. For three years before we came here. But I felt this was where God was directing us. Reece was not so sure." He moved from the desk to stand by the window, looking out. "This is tame for him. A regular church. Regular people."

"No one's regular. We all have problems."

He turned. "I know that. I was raised in church. Do it right. Always smile. Pretend. That kind of church. Not the kind I want. Not the kind God wants. Not the kind Reece would ever do. I couldn't take it anymore, and God did something radical in me. Now, besides Jesus, Reece is the best thing that ever happened to me. He keeps me accountable. I'm not going to lose him, Kati. I refuse. If the devil thinks he's going after Reece, well, he's in for the fight of his life. I was in prayer most of the night last night, and I'm about to do it again. On my face before God. He says come and reason with him. Well, that is just what I'm doing. I'm holding up Reece in prayer, holding up God's promises, and standing against the Evil One."

"Put on the whole armor of God…"

"You got it. Put on the armor, stand, use our weapons, and pray always with all prayer in the spirit." His jaw tightened again, the blue eyes snapped. "Care to join me?"

***

Kati stayed a half hour, then slipped from the room. Joshua could pray for hours. Probably would. But she had to find Reece. It drove her. It was her fault. Joshua hadn't asked again about yesterday, but whatever had sent Reece into a tailspin had started then. Hadn't it?

She texted him as she climbed into her SUV. No answer. She hit the Call button. Nothing.

Where would he go? She had no idea. She headed to his house. Maybe he was home. Twenty minutes later, she sat in her car, looking at the empty house. She'd knocked, and he wasn't there. She glanced at her watch. 5:00 PM. The whole day had passed. When would Joshua leave the office to come home?

She climbed from the Nissan and walked back to the porch. After a moment, she sat on the swing, lifted her phone, and took a selfie.

Her fingers moved over the phone's face. *Reece, I'm waiting for you at your place. Please call or text or come home.* She chewed her lip and sent the text.

An hour later, she'd still heard nothing. Cars had driven up and down the street. People had walked by—no one she recognized. She wondered how Isabella and Manuel were doing. She'd seen them in church last Sunday, knew that Manuel was much better. That had made her day. Now if Reece would just call or text or show, it would be another great day.

She took another selfie, sent it with another text. *I'm still here. Outside on the swing. Waiting.*

Would he show? Would Joshua? As another car went by,

and another face looked her way questioningly, she swallowed. How long should she stay? What if Joshua had a meeting or went to eat with someone?

Sweat rolled down her back, and she walked back to her car, pulled the bottle of warm water from it, and marched back to the porch. At least there was a small breeze. She put her head down and prayed again.

Not like I haven't done this a dozen times since I've been here. Lord, should I go? I don't know how to force his hand. Two boys rushed by, laughing, talking, giving her a sly glance. After a minute, she stood and took another picture—this time of the street. She sent it with the text: *Guess I'll take a walk. Before it gets dark.*

The smell of dinner cooking, the sound of pots and pans knocking together, met her. Someone had a window open, which meant no air conditioner. *Oh, Lord, bring them a breeze. It's hot.*

Her clothes stuck to her body. Perspiration beaded on her forehead. *Wow. I'm in the air conditioning all day, and I've forgotten how hot it is without it.* She took a picture as the lamppost winked on and sent it to Reece.

Where is he, Lord? Please take care of him. Please keep him safe. Please don't let him get involved with anything he shouldn't. Don't let anyone hurt him.

A few minutes later, she wondered if she should turn around and head back. A car turned the corner and headed her way. Lights flashed in her eyes. She moved back from the street, but the car pulled over, stopped. Her stomach clenched. Perhaps this hadn't been a good idea, perhaps…

The door flew outward. She jumped.

"Get in."

"Reece?" Her voice rose.

"Get in, Kati."

"You're here!"

He said nothing. She climbed into the passenger seat and

turned toward him. He pulled on the wheel, doing an overhand as he turned the car around.

"You're being crazy." His voice was hard, muffled.

"Maybe. Maybe not."

"Where's Josh?"

"I don't know."

"You can't wander the streets around here, especially at night."

"It's not night yet."

He threw her a narrow-eyed look.

"Can we talk about the water park?"

"No."

"Can we talk about what's going on with you?"

"No."

"Reece…"

"I'm going to drop you off at your car, and I want you to go home."

"Don't do this, Reece. What's wrong with you? Why are you acting this way?"

His jaw tightened. Emotion flickered over his face.

Kati put a hand on his arm. "Reece, please."

"I can't compare with your boyfriend, Kati. He's Mr. Spiritual, and I'll never measure up to that…holiness."

"Come on, Reece. That's not fair to Joshua. How can you say that?"

He pulled the car over behind hers. "Sorry. Guess it's hard to love him right now. At any rate, I know enough to know I come in second where he's concerned."

"Come in second? What are you talking about? You're never second to anyone. God made each of us special. There's no—"

He grabbed her arm roughly. "I don't want to be 'each of us.' Don't you get that? Don't you understand what I am talking about?"

Her heart blipped at the sound of brokenness in the last sentence. She reached a hand out. "Reece, I—"

He dropped her arm. "Don't, Kati. I don't think I can take you being sorry for me."

"I'm not doing that."

"No?"

He cut the engine off, went round, and opened her door. Kati stepped out, wondering, but he walked her to her car, opened the driver's door, and nodded his head toward it.

"Go home, and don't do this again. I won't be out here to get you again."

She tilted her head back, looking into his eyes. "Reece—"

"You need to back off, Kati, and stay out of the way. I hadn't thought I'd ever feel this way again, but things are spinning out of control. I won't mean to hurt you, but I will. I know myself."

"You know who you used to be."

"Yes. Just that. I know who I was and who I could go back to."

"But you won't."

He stared down at her. "You don't know me. You think you do. Only Josh knows the true me."

"And God."

He drew in a deep breath, let it out. "Go home, Kati."

"No, I—"

He caught her arm again, the grip hurting her. "You don't know what I'm capable of. What I've done."

"It makes no difference. You are who you are now. God has made you brand new."

"If I'm so band new, why do I want to put a few of these guys through a window? Why would I like to go a round with Josh?"

She pulled free, rubbed her arm. "You're jealous of Josh."

His look searched her face, then he reached forward and used a finger to draw a line down her cheek, touched her lips. "Tell me I shouldn't be."

She hesitated. Had she even figured out all the emotions each time either one was near? Why was it so hard? The confusion, the darkness whenever she tried to think it through. "Reece…."

"You can't, can you?" He backed away, turned.

"Reece, please."

He rounded on her, the pain in his eyes raw and alive. "Leave me alone, Kati."

"No, I—"

"You want to know who I am? A gang member, that's who. I knew who those guys were the minute they pulled to the curb that day. I had to find my Glock because I didn't know how violent they might be. The gang I was with was violent. There were only a few of us with a Welsh background, and we thought we had to be violent to survive. I was an enforcer. Do you know what an enforcer is? I hurt people with my fists. That's why I won't go into the ring with you or anyone down there. I've been there, and it wasn't for fun." His voice was hard. He was still hurting her, but with his words now.

"You were…what?"

"Yeah, an enforcer. I've never killed anyone. Told them I wouldn't do that, but for years I messed people over."

"You don't do that anymore."

"No, but I wanted to. When he looked at you, when he held the gun to Pedro's head, I felt it. The darkness was there, waiting."

She leaned forward. "You are not that person anymore."

"Are you sure? Because I'm not."

"I am." She straightened herself, met his gaze unwaveringly.

He kept her gaze for a long moment, then turned and walked back to his Range Rover, started the engine, and roared past her.

***

128

The Bible sat open on her desk. The music, the hour-long praise and worship, had died. Still the heaviness remained, the whirring inside.

Who do I think I am, praying as if it would lift whatever stronghold has gripped Reece? Who am I, anyway? Someone who ran from church, from God when my world exploded. Instead of to Him, I ran away. Yeah to another church, but one where they knew nothing about me, where they required nothing of me.

Of course, through the last couple of years, she'd begun to do things around the church, work her way back to that place in God she'd called home before. Pastor Alan and Miss Eleanor had gently encouraged her to pray, to seek God. And now Joshua and Reece had come. God was doing something, and he had called her into it. She knew it.

The roar in her head increased. Darkness hovered, perched near her. She squinted and shook her head and nearly laughed. For a moment, she'd seen something like bats flying around her head. *Right. Sure. It's just a headache.*

"But I never have headaches." Her voice was low. Tears formed, slid down her cheeks.

Lord, please help Reece. Don't let him slip through.

Kati paced back and forth in the bedroom, then the hall and ended in the kitchen. The shadows pressed in. She'd only left one light on in the house—the one in the bedroom. The windows didn't just yawn but instead gaped like wide mouths. She closed her eyes, fought the desire to run back to the bedroom.

No. No, she wouldn't do that. Reece had called her a warrior, and if Joshua could do battle, then she could, too.

Outside, a dog howled. She shivered, then bowed her head. *Reece needs you, Lord. He needs you now. Just as Ryann does. Don't let the Enemy lie to him, to them. Whatever he did before is forgiven, in the past, dead. He's a new creature. Remind him of that.* Kati brought her head up. *And so am I. I might have run before, but I'm not going to now. Whatever you have for us, Father, I want it. I want you. Help me do battle.*

She picked up her Bible, flipped to 2 Corinthians 10:4. "The weapons of our warfare are mighty through God to the pulling down of strongholds."

"You hear that, Enemy?" She said aloud, rising and straightening her shoulders. "Reece is a new creature in Christ. Old things are passed away. All things are new." She waited a moment. "I stand against whatever lies are attacking Reece. I stand in the gap for Reece. Lord, please reach him. Open his eyes and ears to you."

She spun around, finger pointed. "You that aren't of God, go. In the name of Jesus, go! Stop your lies. The enemies of God are released from their assignment against him. Go! He belongs to Jesus. Go!"

Silence. She closed her eyes, standing, waiting, and then she ran to the bedroom, grabbed the speaker hooked to her laptop, and punched the sound as high as it would go. The worship song flung sound across the room, through the house. She went through each room and turned on the lights, then sank to her knees.

"Reece is under the blood. He's a soldier in the Lord's army, no one else's. King of kings, Lord of lords, he belongs to you."

***

Reece drove to the other side of town. No use letting someone from the church or the neighborhood see him. All he wanted was a drink…or two. Anything to get the taste of Kati's and Josh's words out of his mouth. Or maybe his own. He slumped in the seat.

He just couldn't do this. Yeah, he'd done it for three years, but this new place, these people, even Kati—how could he compare to all their good deeds? He didn't have good deeds. In the old neighborhood, everyone knew him, even the different gangs. They could see he'd changed. But here? He was just a rough stone here, out of place.

You also, as a living stone, are being built up into a spiritual house, a holy priesthood.

He sighed. His chest heaved. He dropped his head for a second, then jerked it back to watch the road.

"What kind of stone can I be here? These people are rubies and diamonds. Think of Rich Richards and his wife, and Jake and China, and Miss Eleanor. Their lives imitated Christ's. Had for years. Who am I?" The words echoed in the SUV.

He pulled into the bar's parking lot, cut the engine, and stared. He hadn't had a drink since he'd accepted Christ into his life.

Just get out and go in. You'll feel better. No one to judge you in there. No one wanting you to do better.

It is through grace you are saved by faith and that not of yourself. It is the gift of God.

Could he shut up the Bible verses? Another thing Josh had insisted on. Memorize Scripture. Take it with you. Yeah. And you couldn't get rid of it when you wanted to.

A picture of Kati coming down a slide at the park leapt to his mind. He couldn't help a smile. Her laughter, the way her hair spiked when she came out of the water and shook it. The bathing suit. All right. It was modest, but it fit like a second skin, and there was more bare skin than he'd seen before. She did all sorts of things to him. Made him feel like he was someone.

His jaw tightened. That was the problem. She didn't know who he was. He bet if he told her some actual stories of what his life had been like three years ago, she'd run like a cheetah away from him.

Another car pulled into the parking lot, and a girl and a man climbed out. They circled each other's waist with their arms, laughing, and went inside.

131

That was what he needed. A woman who'd come here with him. Once in a while. They wouldn't do it every week. Just when life threw them curves. Like tonight.

He climbed from the SUV. The voices in his mind wouldn't shut up. He lowered his head, swung it back and forth to rid it of the confusion.

"Wondered if you were ever getting out."

The voice jumped at him, and he spun around.

Terry smirked. "What? You don't bring Kati to the bars?"

A sledgehammer couldn't have created more damage. Reece's heart collapsed with the force of the blow.

The gym owner's smirk turned into a look of triumph. "On the other side of town so no one will see you? Don't worry. I won't tell."

Reece couldn't find his voice, couldn't think of anything to say.

"You might find a woman inside, too." Terry motioned with his head. "One that's not so straight laced and hands off." He chuckled and walked toward the bar's door.

Which was just what Reece had wanted, until now. His lip curled. He didn't want what Terry wanted. He didn't want a one-night stand. Not anymore. He wasn't adverse to marriage. It was just the marriages he'd seen had gone sour quickly.

But God...

Josh said there were no guarantees, but finding someone who had a commitment to God and a commitment to marriage would make its success a better bet. And Kati had both. He was sure. Then he closed his eyes. But she was Josh's. Maybe Josh didn't see it yet. Or Kati. Reece's memory of her in his arms, her response to his kiss, rushed back.

The blackness hovered. He could see it now. See the way it waited for him to give in to the depression, the sense of worthlessness, of never being enough.

You are redeemed by the blood of the Lamb, not of works...
It is by grace.

132

Josh had preached grace to him that first year. Over and over.

Why now did it seem like he had to live perfectly? He inhaled, put his hand to the side of the car so his knees wouldn't buckle.

God, I'm not good for this. Why did you call us here? These people are decent and moral. His mind jumped to the prayer walk. Many in the congregation had gone, but they'd been scared. Scared of the people in the neighborhood. His mouth hitched. As if those in a lower economic condition were any different from their middle-class lives. They had the same struggles, the same loves, the same battles against sickness, the same fights to pay the bills. Yes, maybe more so in the lower-income community, but he'd seen how middle-class families still fought to pay bills after they'd bought too much, spent too much on vacation or Christmas. They still had children to raise, sickness to overcome, jobs to get up for each day...

The men and women of the church just needed to know... The swirling around him slowed. *Is this why I'm here? Is this...* His brain cleared. Light poured in. Knowledge. Revelation.

He owed Josh an apology. God an apology.

He glanced up. "I ask forgiveness for my orneriness, for my blindness about this whole thing. I didn't want to come, didn't see the vision. Now I do."

And Kati...

His chest constricted. He'd have to make that sacrifice. He would have done that anyway. He'd never do anything to hurt Josh. He looked at the bar again, at the flickering lights, the window signs.

Thank you, Terry, for showing up here. For saying what you did. Save that man, God. Bring him to you. Reece nodded. Maybe he'd have to get back in the ring again. Not to win a fight, but to win a soul. He took a deep breath. If he had to...

Josh was right. This was a life and death battle, not a sporting match. Even if Josh wasn't Mr. Perfect. For Reece, Josh came close. But it wasn't for Josh that Reece lived his life. It was for Christ.

And he'd almost stepped back into the cauldron Jesus had pulled him from. His thoughts bounced from one idea to another. He'd given in to the devil these last couple of days, sinking into self-pity, condemnation, worthlessness. All lies. He was a new creature. He was born again.

Set your face like flint.

He climbed back into the SUV. "I am a child of God. I belong to him. I will live for him." The words vibrated throughout the SUV. He nodded, said them again, and shoved the gears into reverse.

***

Kati trotted around the corner of the Life Center. Josh had called to say that Reece was back. Her heart tripped. Her eyes watered. She just wanted to see him. Her feet slowed. Maybe running over to see him after their discussion last night might not be a good idea.

She'd prayed and praised the Lord all night, her heart torn for Reece. He meant so much to her. Everything in her wanted to run into his arms, but how could she? After last night... Yes, Joshua meant a lot to her, but Reece did too.

Why this confusion, Lord?

She stopped at the door to office. Maybe he wasn't here. Maybe he, or he and Josh, had gone somewhere. She hesitated. She hadn't told Joshua she was coming, hadn't asked if he or Reece was busy. She took a step back.

The door opened. She jumped.

Reece had his head turned, looking over his shoulder. He said something to China. The girl laughed, and Reece twisted back Kati's way. Stopped.

They stared at each other. Kati felt her mouth open. Hope leapt into her chest. He looked good. The darkness from yesterday had vanished. She couldn't think of anything to say.

"Hello, Kati."

"Hi." Another pause. "Reece, I...I..."

"I'm sorry about last night." He seemed embarrassed, tongue tied. "I mean, I—"

She tried to hold back, tried not to throw herself at him, but she couldn't help wrapping her arms around him. "You're back!"

His body went rigid, and then he gave in to the hug and squeezed her gently, as if she were one of those foil sculptures you could crush in one hand, and then he extricated himself from her hold.

His shoulders straightened. His mouth formed a small smile. "I couldn't let Josh stay on his knees forever."

She giggled. "Well, good."

"God is bigger than my...stupidity."

"Will you stop? You are not stupid. He's called you. You have a purpose."

He nodded. "He wants me for some reason." The brief smile again. "So, Satan has lost an accomplice." He headed down the steps.

"Reece."

The hesitation was noticeable. He glanced at her, his face shuttered. "Yes?"

"Josh told me you were here."

His brows lifted, but he said nothing.

"I...I wanted to see you."

His head dipped.

What was she doing? *Kati, you fool. Leave him alone. Leave them both alone.* Her face must have reflected some emotion, because he turned fully and studied her.

"I'm going to a Christian concert Friday night. Do you...would you like to go?"

Her heart dropped. Why was this happening? "I can't."

The shuttered eyes returned. "Okay."

"Joshua…asked me already. When he called about you. He asked then. I…"

"It's all right, Kati. I understand. Maybe I'll see you there." This time the turn and the movement down the steps were quick and firm.

Her throat constricted; her chest pounded. *Oh, Reece.* She wanted to run after him, to tell him she'd changed her mind, that she'd tell Joshua no, but she didn't have the courage or the surety that it was right.

She dropped her head. *God, I need you to remove this confusion from me. I've never been in a place like this before. Take away the indecision, and let me, let my heart, know which of these men you've chosen for me.* She raised her head and looked skyward. *If…it's either of them.*

Chapter 9

Then [the angel] said to me, "Do not fear, Daniel, for from the
first day that you set your heart to understand, and to humble
yourself before your God, your words were heard; and I have
come because of your words."
(Daniel 10:12 NKJV)

People filled the venue grounds. The concert had numerous celebrated Christian artists and thousands of attendees. Kati loved the songs lifted up to God. Her initial tension about seeing Reece while with Joshua faded as they sang, laughed, and praised God together.

Late-afternoon shadows crawled toward their camp chairs. A soft wind helped counter the warmth and humidity. Joshua had scouted the area beforehand and found one of the rare places with shade. Many of the attendees, though, had their own canopies.

The break between sessions wouldn't last long, and Kati wondered if they'd try to get something to eat and drink.

Joshua stood and stretched. "This has been good, Kati."

She stood too, along with many others around them. "Thank you for asking me."

He dipped his head. She stared. If it wasn't ridiculous, she'd think he'd looked embarrassed for a moment. "I knew you'd enjoy it."

"I have." She swept her hand to all the people surrounding them. "Just as everyone has."

Joshua turned in a slow circle. "It's become packed, hasn't it?"

"Yes."

"Do you mind grabbing us some drinks? I know you'll hit the lines, but…" He stumbled over the word. "But there's a friend I'd really like to talk to." He looked over her head in the opposite direction of the food tents.

She slid a glance in the direction he was looking but only saw a multitude of people moving around. "Sure, I…sure. What do you want?"

He pulled some cash from his pocket. "I'll do a bottle of water and anything you want to eat. Grab whatever you want." His eyes went over her head again.

She took the money. "Okay, but I hope you like it."

His gaze dropped to hers. "Anything, Kati, really." He turned and strode away.

She stopped trying to watch his tall figure after a minute. *Strange.* But then a pastor had plenty of people that needed his attention… She started in the other direction.

Children ran in front of her. Someone played their own guitar now that the music had stopped. Grass and sand made up the concert's outside venue. The food tents were on the opposite side. She'd be hot and dirty when she made it there and back. Oh well…

Reece stood in front of her, half turned away, his head bent, listening to the woman who clung to his arm. Kati's steps faltered.

The woman's long honey-colored hair highlighted her dark eyes and wide lips. A black formfitting jacket topped a pair of tight jeans and T-shirt.

Kati's body went cold. She stopped. Perhaps she'd go around…

Reece raised his head. A startled look passed over his face, and his mouth pulled tight.

Kati's chest emptied. He didn't want to see her. She

dropped her head, wondering how to avoid them.

"Hello, Kati." The words were stiff.

She brought her head up and took a hesitant step in his direction. "Hi, Reece."

The girl moved closer to him, and he glanced at her. "Salome, this is Kati, a friend of mine. Kati, Salome."

The women nodded at each other. A friend. That was all Kati was. All she'd ever be if things continued as is. The sickness in her stomach climbed high.

Reece's head moved right and left. "Where's Josh?"

"I don't know for sure." Kati shrugged. "He said he had to speak with someone and sent me to get drinks."

Reece straightened, looked over the field again. "Well, let him know we're here, will you?"

"Sure. Of course." Kati forced a smile. *But I hope we don't do a foursome.*

"You hungry, Salome? Let's get something."

The woman wrapped her hands around Reece's arm. "Sure, sweetie. It smells good."

Kati was going to gag. Yep. Gag. If her heart didn't hurt so much, she just might do it here. She turned away, stared at the empty stage, trying to keep her face from revealing the pain shooting through her. She couldn't focus on anything. She fought the tears in her throat and waited until Reece and Salome had time to get lost in the crowd, before weaving her way to the food tents.

It hadn't taken Reece long to ask someone else to the concert. He'd sounded so sincere the other night, as if she truly meant something to him. She pushed the feelings down. *Don't go there, Kati. You said no. Of course he asked someone else.* She bit her lip. Where did he meet her? Someone in the neighborhood? He certainly hadn't asked Kati back to his house again.

Stop! Stop, Kati. The Enemy is having a field day with you. She raised her head. Okay. Food. Drinks.

Maybe a bathroom?

Yeah. Find a bathroom and calm down. She neared one end of the food tents. There must be portable potties nearby. Kati came around the corner and leaned against the wooden fence at the back of the tents. Sweat rolled down her back. She rubbed her hands on her jean shorts. They'd have sinks and hopefully soap, too.

Movement to her right caught her attention. Reece, again. Kati froze. He stood not far away, talking to Ryann's boyfriend. Kati frowned. Was Ryann here, too?

Reece pulled some bills from his pocket, folded them, and handed them to the other man. Kati stared but didn't move. She surveyed the area around them. No one else was near.

Landon squinted past Reece, his face tight. Kati sank back. Landon handed Reece a small packet.

What was going on? They were not....no!

Kati straightened and darted forward. "Hey!"

Both men whirled her way.

"Reece! What are you doing? Are you crazy?" She ran the last few feet and grabbed at the packet in his hand.

His eyes rounded, but he yanked his hand back. "Kati, what are you—"

Landon jerked a look at Reece, then whirled and fled.

"Give me that. Do you hear me?" She grabbed at his hand again. "I don't know what you think you're doing, but—"

Salome and a deputy ran by them. Kati's head shot up, and she watched them disappear around a group of people, following Landon.

A second later, Rich skidded to a stop. "What's she doing here? She ruined the whole thing."

"No, she hasn't. She—"

"Ruined what?" Kati stared at Rich.

"Maybe. Maybe not. What are you doing, Kati? Where's Josh?"

"No idea. He left to talk with someone." She glared at

Reece. "What is going on with you?"

"What did you think?"

"I thought…" She glanced from him to Rich, confusion rising inside.

"You thought I was buying drugs?"

"Well…yeah. That's what it looked like. What were you doing?"

"Helping us." Rich let loose an exasperated breath. "Joshua was supposed to keep Ryann out of the way. And you, too. Where is he?"

Reece gave a snort. "Probably found someone to minister to."

Kati let her focus shift from one to the other. "You mean *Landon* is a drug dealer?"

"She's got it."

"And you weren't buying drugs?"

"Not for real, no."

"And this whole…you being so down…that was part of it?"

Reece shifted. "Yeah."

She stood on tiptoe and got in his face. "Liar."

Rich cleared his throat. "What is she talking about?"

"Nothing."

Kati leaned in, nose to nose. "If you're not lying, then I just spent some radical time in prayer a few days ago that was a total waste of time."

She spun and stalked back the way she'd come. The man—no, men—were driving her crazy. Had Reece been playing a role this whole time? Had her emotional prayers been a mockery? And what about Joshua? Where was he?

She rounded the fence like a thoroughbred at the Kentucky Derby. Her teeth ground. And Reece had asked her to come with him. What would he have done with her while he was pretend-buying drugs? Same thing he'd done with Salome. No…Salome must be a cop. She'd run by them with the deputy, going after Landon.

Kati skidded to a stop. *Landon sold drugs!*

Something hit her from behind. She lurched forward. A hand grabbed her arm and yanked her upright. "Hey!"

Reece turned her to face him. "Sorry. I couldn't stop that fast."

"Landon is a drug dealer?"

"Yes."

"But what about Ryann? She doesn't…"

"Have anything to do with it. In fact, she told Joshua the day you tried to talk to her. Remember? You came rushing out of the church after her, and I stopped you."

"You did. I was so mad."

"You were gonna fight me."

She crossed her arms. "You mean you guys knew then? About the drugs?"

"Josh did. She wanted out of the relationship, but Landon threatened her. Said she'd never leave him. Alive." Reece's tone had deepened. "Guys like him are hard to love."

Things stopped inside her. Yes, they were. *They are, Lord.* "So this whole thing—"

"Was what Rich and Josh and the Sheriff's Office put together to get Landon."

"Did I ruin it?" She clasped her head with her hands. "Please tell me I didn't ruin it."

"Kati, it's all right. We'd made the exchange."

"Yeah. Yeah, you did. I was so angry when I saw that."

He chuckled. "I got that."

She huffed. "So all this…this…you being down was an act?"

The smile vanished. "No. It wasn't. If you prayed, then your prayers worked. I finally saw through the haze. Saw that God had me here for a reason. That I'm not…worthless."

"Worthless?" She stared at him. *What?* "Please tell me you know you're *priceless*."

He snorted. "Christ is. Only him, but I'm in Him, and I'll stick with that." He glanced over his shoulder. "Look, I've got to get back. If you can, find Josh and Ryann and let them know what's up. But don't let Ryann out of your sight until we hear whether Landon is in custody or not."

***

Kati wandered in the direction from which she'd come, but her mind was on Reece. The complete plunge in her heart when she'd thought he was buying drugs still drifted through her emotions. Like when they'd talked the other night, when he'd seemed so lost to her. How had he come to mean so much to her in such a short amount of time?

She heard Joshua's voice, sounding hard and inflexible. She jerked her head around. *Joshua's voice?*

He stood close to a large man with a belligerent smirk, eyes screwed up. Ryann stood behind Joshua, face white. A couple of other people looked on. What was happening?

Joshua leaned forward. "You've obviously had too many beers or something. Why don't you walk it off? Just leave the lady alone."

The man shoved Joshua back a foot. "I was talking to the *lady*, not you. Bug off."

"Well, the lady doesn't want your attentions, and she's with me now." He turned to Ryann. "Let's go get those drinks."

The man grabbed Joshua's arm and yanked him back around. "Like I said before, you need to bug off."

Joshua stared at him. "Take your hands off me."

"Yeah. I'd rather have them on the little lady here anyway. You know what I mean, pal?"

Ryann's face blanched.

Kati stepped next to her. "Are you okay?"

Ryann shook her head. "Joshua was supposed to meet me here a while ago, but this...this guy was bugging me, so I left.

143

Then when I came back, he started all over again. He wouldn't leave me alone."

Joshua snatched his arm free from the man's grip. "I'm sure there's a policeman around somewhere. If you aren't gone in a minute, I'll find one."

"Can't fight your own battles? You always run home to mama, or maybe you want to get into this lady's pants more than I do?"

Joshua's fist connected with the man's jaw.

The man stumbled backward, eyes rounding. "Why you…" A line of curse words flew forth even as his fist connected with Joshua's face.

Joshua spun from the hit, and blood pooled on his lip. Ryann screamed. The man leapt forward, a meaty hand slamming Joshua's jaw. Joshua staggered backward again but managed to keep his feet under him.

Kati didn't think. She jumped toward the man and sent a roundhouse kick to his side. He yowled and twisted away. A moment later, he whirled back around, fists swinging. Kati bobbed back, then leaned in and sent a jab to his face, followed by a left hook kick. He tried to grab her kick and missed. Snarling like a bull, he put his head down and charged her. Joshua hit him from the side. Both men tumbled to the ground. People began to yell, and someone pulled the big man off Josh, but he broke free and lunged at Kati. She sidestepped, then swung round and downed him with an uppercut.

"All right, police! Police! Break it up. Break it up."

Kati's wrist was grabbed, and someone spun her around. Right before she sent a jab to her attacker's face, she saw the uniform.

***

Joshua threw the door open to their house. "Reece, all right, man. Enough."

Reece stumbled in behind him, hand on his stomach. His laughter made Joshua cringe.

"Are you kidding? Your first month on the job, and you're arrested. You. Arrested. For throwing a punch."

"It's past the first-month mark."

"Oh. Excuse me. The two-month mark." Reece's grin was wicked.

"If it wasn't for Kati, you could laugh all you wanted, but I got her arrested."

Reece's grin lowered. He shook his head. "I could lay into you for that, but even Kati said you didn't know she was there. And she would have loved to kayo the guy. I'm glad we got to take her home, talk to her."

Joshua went to the refrigerator, grabbed a Coke, and sat at the table. "Yeah. In spite of the bravado, she was shaken. I can't believe she got arrested because of me."

"Dude, I can't believe *you* got arrested. Kati seemed proud of herself."

Joshua eyed him, shook his head. "Poor girl. And it'll be on the news."

"Pastor at New Life Church in Concert Brawl." Reece laughed again. "You'd better call Pastor Alan. Oh. And Miss Eleanor." He tilted his head. "Before she sees the news."

Joshua's face changed. He fingered his lip, pulled back from the pain, and rolled his eyes. "Miss Eleanor. And the church." He groaned. "You know this was easier on the streets with just you and me. They could insult us all they wanted, but when that dude started in with smack about Ryann, I saw red. No, make that crimson, volcanic fire."

Reece let his smile hover. "Crimson. As in football? The Crimson Tide?"

"No, bro. The color. Or maybe yeah. Yeah. The Crimson Tide and how I wanted to overrun him."

"I guess we better order out."

"What?"

"Order out. You know. I'm hungry, and if we go anywhere, someone might ask for your autograph."

Joshua groaned again.

"Don't worry about it, bro. You and Kati will probably only draw community service, and Sunday's service will be the most packed out yet."

***

Arrested.

Kati stepped from her living room to the back deck and stared at the moonlight. Wow. What a ride. Not all good, but she was certainly out of the safe zone.

She walked farther onto her deck, stared up at the full moon. The scenes from today played over in her head. Reece with Salome, Reece buying drugs, Joshua handcuffed and being put in the police cruiser. Her own ride in a police cruiser. *A holding cell.*

As disconcerting as it all was, it didn't compare to the lurch of her heart when Reece had said he wasn't worthless. Why had he ever thought that? Couldn't he see his own strength, his courage, his caring, his worth in Christ?

Every time she was near him, her own courage grew—as if he was imparting some of his to her. Like Jesus did. That was what was happening. The presence of Christ in Reece overflowed to those around him, just as Joshua's did. Just as it should from her.

The wind wove the fragrance of jasmine around her. She smiled and sat on one of the deck chairs. Trees stood black against a dark sky. The beauty around her awed her.

"I wish Reece were here." She remembered the fierceness of his kiss, his laughter, his protectiveness. And his anger when he'd arrived at the police station to bail her out. And Josh. For a moment, she had thought he'd hit Joshua and they'd all be back in jail. But the anger passed quickly, and once he knew

146

she was okay, he'd begun to laugh. Hadn't stopped even after they had dropped her off. She'd heard him ribbing Joshua again as they backed out of her drive.

Lord, I've been so stupid. I love Reece. I love Josh's spirituality, but Reece is spiritual, too. It's just in a different way. He's not perfect, no, but neither am I. Far from it, but I think he loves me, or at least cares a lot. She hugged herself tighter. *I'm scared, Lord. I don't want to hurt their friendship. What am I going to do?*

Chapter 10

Trust in the Lord with all your heart and lean not unto your own understanding. In all your ways acknowledge him, and he shall direct your path.
(Proverbs 3:5–6 NKJV)

The church was filled to capacity. Ryann sat on her left, and Kati felt the rush of thanksgiving about it. Even if she was still miffed at Ryann insisting she couldn't confide in her.

"Kati, I couldn't. As soon as you saw Landon, he would have known I'd told you."

"I can keep a secret," Kati contended. "I wouldn't have said anything."

"You wouldn't, but your *face* would have."

Kati leaned back in the pew. It was all good. Ryann was free now, free to see her friends, free to come to church, maybe free to seek out Matt again. Who knew?

She glanced at the vacant seat on her right. Usually Miss Eleanor sat there, but today she was near the back with her daughter. Her daughter had left church some years ago. Was she was back today because of the publicity?

Kati smiled. *Well, Lord, whatever it takes to get them here.*

Lots of noise, talking, whispering, even laughter had accompanied the people filling the sanctuary, but it faded when the music minister stepped forward. The first song dropped an anointing so strong that it felt like warm oil poured over them.

Thick. That was the only way she could describe it. An atmosphere so thick with God's love that the talking, the whispering, the shifting in the pews had ceased.

Joshua stepped to the pulpit a moment later to pray, then asked Manny to continue with the worship songs.

Kati sat back in the pew and bowed her head. *Lord, I need you. I love you.*

As the music ended a second time, no one moved. A sense of awe filled the place. On the platform, the worship team all had their eyes closed. Joshua knelt beside the pulpit, head bent.

Kati could hear prayers all around her. She added her own. *Lord, light the fire in me again. Make me different. Give me courage. Let me love others more than myself.*

In a few minutes, Joshua stood and clicked on his microphone. "I know many have come today for different reasons, but we're going to let God have his way today. I'm not going to preach unless I feel his urging, and at this moment, I don't. I do, however, feel that someone's heart is being touched by God. If that's you, let him have his way. This is a safe place. Let God heal whatever hurt you've been dealing with."

Kati's chest squeezed. Tears started. She couldn't stop them. Why couldn't she get rid of the shame and the guilt? It wasn't hers. She knew that in her head, but… She stood up, heart pounding like a bell pealing, dong, dong, dong, one that all could hear.

Joshua's eyes met hers. "Kati?"

The quiet around her increased. She could hear the listening congregation. *Lord…* Perspiration dotted her body.

"My parents died in an auto accident." She'd never told anyone here.

Joshua's eyes filled with compassion. He nodded.

"They…they were pillars of the church we attended. Everyone loved them. But no one knew that my father drank, that…we were afraid of him, of his anger, his drinking. I don't know how he kept it secret so long. He'd drink and rave at us, then pass out at night. He never hit us, but we were so afraid.

His yelling. His intimidation."

She dropped her head, hesitated, felt the well of tears, and forced them down. "He was driving my mother to see her dad in the hospital. An emergency, so my dad had no time to sober up, and of course he insisted on driving. He…he ran off the road." The thickness in the atmosphere increased. "They were killed instantly. The cause of the accident came out in the news. I…I was so ashamed. People in the church were shocked. No one knew what to say. I didn't know what to say. They thought my dad was such a strong Christian. And in some ways he was. But he drank every day, and mom and I hid it, had never told anyone. Attending church became hard after that, so awkward. Finally, I just left, moved here. For the last three years, I've been here. Afraid to let anyone know. I…I started kickboxing because I knew I needed my courage back. I thought it would help. But I want my joy back, too, and the enthusiasm I used to have for God."

She sat back down, closed her eyes. Music started again. The love was palpable, like a heavy blanket wrapping itself around her, around the whole place. Ryann's hand covered hers where it rested on the pew, squeezed. In a moment, someone sat beside her. No words, no touch. Just there. She opened her eyes, slid a glance to her left. Reece sat there, head bowed. Her heart swelled.

Another hand touched her shoulder. "Kati." Josh's voice. "I'm sorry about your parents. They were too young to die. You were too young to have it happen. Thank you for being open and vulnerable with us. But realize that what your father did has nothing to do with you. You have no guilt in that. And remember that no one is perfect. Your father wasn't, but it seems he raised you in church, and for that you can be thankful. Thank God for that and forgive your father. Forgive those in the church that might have done or said wrong things about it. You were wounded and hurt and did not have anyone to stand in the gap for you. We will. We will now."

He lifted his head. "I want anyone who feels led to come here and help us pray for Kati, to lift the burden of guilt from her, to ask God to give her the ability to forgive her father, to return her joy and courage to her. Come now."

Sometime later, she sat head bowed again. Others had stood to give a testimony or repent of things they'd done or just ask for prayer for family members, and now everyone sat quiet. Joshua still hadn't preached. Expectancy filled the church. Kati felt it.

Not what, Lord?

Near the back, a throat cleared. Another testimony? She lifted her head, glanced around. At the back, Miss Eleanor stood.

The octogenarian straightened. "This is a change from what's going on, but I think it's necessary." Her eyes focused on Joshua. "If we put aside what happened at that…concert…for now, we still have something else to deal with. There's talk of another prayer walk. I would like to know how you plan on keeping the people safe after what happened last time."

Joshua inclined his head. "Miss Eleanor, you and I had this conversation before. It's a very pertinent question. We've prayed together about this, for the church, and for God's will to be done."

"Yes, we have."

He moved to the pulpit and glanced over the congregation. "How many others have this same concern?"

Kati glanced around. Hands went up throughout the sanctuary.

"When I came here, I knew we could not do what God put on my heart without a fight. Satan was not going to sit still while we invaded the neighborhood nearby to tell them about Christ, to reach out to them, to bring help and healing."

In the back, a man stood. "We're not so much worried about Satan, Pastor, as about the gang members."

A ripple of laughter rose.

Joshua laughed with the others, then grew serious. "I understand those sentiments. However, you know and I know that God tells us we do not fight against flesh and blood." He raised a hand. "It was definitely flesh and blood that held a gun to Pedro's head, but the instigation for that action comes from the Enemy. We might say we believe in angels and demons, but do we really? The Gospels are full of Jesus' dealing with demons. And those enemy forces are still here today. Likewise, angelic forces are, too. In Hebrews, it talks explicitly that angels are here to help those that will be heirs to the kingdom of God. That's us."

"Well, we certainly needed those angels last time."

"And we had them. We'd all spent time in prayer about the walk. If we hadn't done that, then we would have had need to worry." He took a deep breath. "But this battle is not without casualties. You know most of the New Testament disciples were martyred. In a war, there are casualties. I don't think it is any different in the battle we're in. Satan takes out people when he can." He tilted his head in Kati's direction. "He tried to take out Kati after the death of her parents. She was wounded, but not destroyed. She's still here. Still doing battle, whether she realizes it or not. Her encouragement to me since I've been here has kept me focused, steady. I believe that as we pray, hold forth the name of Jesus, and God's Word, that we will unleash spiritual forces to fight on our behalf. We see battle in the heavens in the book of Daniel."

"That's in the Old Testament."

"So it is, but if you look at Revelation in the New Testament, you see that same battle. Angels and demons. Good versus evil. What you need to do is go home and pray. Is this what God wants you to do? And if so, are you willing to fight, to pray, to love others even if it means someone might get hurt? Even die?"

"That's a lot you're asking, Pastor."

Joshua nodded. "Yes, it is."

Kati forced herself from her seat. Joshua lifted a brow at her. She turned with her back to him and faced the congregation. "I've heard all of your talk about what happened a few weeks ago. I've heard your fear and your concern. And you just heard how fear ruled my life. But we can't let that happen. Are we just going to sit here when people need help? Or they overdose? Or die without God? Or are we going to follow the vision God has given Joshua? Because it's not just for him. It's our vision, too. What are we going to do with it?"

Beside her, Reece stood. "When you went out prayer-walking the first time, you went in fear, but also in obedience. Now the danger's increased. It's real, and it's time to decide what you're about—or more pointedly—what your Christianity is about. Is it about tickling your ears with what you want to hear, or making your life more comfortable, or giving yourself more stuff? Or is it about saving lives? There are people out there no different from you—except for their circumstances. Will you ignore them? Pretend they don't exist while you go home to your big-screen TVs and your backyard barbeques? Or are you going to reach out and love someone?" His eyes raked every part of the sanctuary, touched each person. "Do you know the God you serve, this Creator you give lip service to, do you know his love and his power? If God be God, then serve Him, but if not, serve Baal. It's time to stop playing church and *be* the Church."

He sat down. Kati stared. Wow. A thousand hoofbeats drummed in her chest.

Pedro rose. "I have a wife, a child on the way. I do not want to die." He paused. "But I do not want to displease my God either. Pastor Alan gave me a job when no one else would. He told me about Christ. Jesus has changed my life. How can I not do that for someone else? Do what Pastor Alan did for me? What Pastor Josh is asking us to do?" He looked around, his eyes narrowed. "Are we so scared for our own lives that we would not risk them for someone else's?"

Joshua stood at the pulpit but said nothing. Only his whispered prayer rose. "Your will, Lord. Your will."

The sound of rain started, grew. Kati looked toward the side door. She saw nothing through the glass window. She glanced heavenward. The sound of rain increased, clanging in her mind. Like chains. The rain and the sound of chains falling filled the church. She twisted in her seat. Was she the only one who heard it? Faces turned up to heaven or bent toward the floor, eyes closed. She shook her head. Prayers started somewhere behind her, multiplied, grew, the sound an extension of the rain.

She bowed her head. Chains breaking. Rain falling. The Holy Spirit doing His work in her heart, in others' hearts.

Joshua's voice rose above the others. "Lord, we hear you. Yours is the kingdom, yours is the glory. Freedom is coming. Strongholds are breaking. Form us now into a mighty army. Warriors. Call us. Equip us. Take these dry bones and put flesh on them. Put your Spirit in us. Send us. Hear am I, Lord. Use me."

Others began to repeat the words. Kati muttered them under her breath, then louder. "Hear am I, Lord. Use me. Use me."

***

Another hour had passed before she made her way to the sanctuary doors. Others had trickled out, going home over the last half hour, but Kati had wanted to absorb all she could of God's presence. Not that he wasn't there all the time, but the corporate worship had held such a tangible feel of his presence.

She stepped outside and almost ran into Reece. His eyes filled with warmth. She froze under their scrutiny.

"Thank you for saying what you did, Kati. I love your courage—whether you realize you have it or not." He smiled, made a quick turn, and headed down the steps to the parking lot.

She stared after him. Was God giving her a chance to tell Reece how she felt? She pushed by someone in front of her and hurried after him. He crossed the parking lot to his SUV. Kati followed.

"Reece."

He turned, but his eyes no longer held the warmth they had a moment before. His face had settled into a mask. She caught her breath at the change.

"I don't have much time, Kati. I've got a meeting. Something I can't miss."

The people who had stayed to the end were getting in their cars and leaving. Only a few cars remained in the parking lot, and he'd parked away from the others as usual. Courage. He'd said she had courage. *For once, let it be true.*

"Okay." She swallowed. "I just wanted to say that I know now. I know I love you. I had some back and forth, that's true, but that was ridiculous stuff. Forgive me. I...I just wanted you to know that I love you."

He stilled, stared down at her, said nothing.

"Reece." Her heart caved. Was it too late? Maybe he didn't feel the same. Maybe she'd just imagined it. She reached out, stopped. "I..."

"Because things are dangerous? Because something could happen to me?"

Alarm skittered across her chest. "What are you talking about?"

"This meeting..." His eyes darkened. "Think about what you're saying, Kati. Think about Josh."

She threw her hands out. "I'm not talking about Josh. I'm talking about you. I love *you*. I thought you..." She stepped back, the beating inside her chest so erratic, so hard that she dropped her head. She'd thought he loved her. She thought that was what he meant the other day... Her head came up, and she met his look. "Whether or not you feel the same, I'm not sorry

LINDA K. RODANTE

I said it. It's true."

"Kati." The huskiness of his voice sent waves of emotion through her. "Are you sure?"

She nodded. His gaze seemed to penetrate hers, searching. She swallowed again and tried to fight back the tears gathering in her throat.

With a groan, his arms drew her to him, enfolded her, and crushed her. His mouth descended on hers, ardent and bruising. Pent-up emotions soared and echoed through her.

It was minutes before they parted.

Joy soared through her. She drew a finger over his lips. "I love you."

He closed his eyes, kissed the tips of her fingers. "Why?"

"Why?"

"Yes, you could have Josh. I know his feelings for you. He—"

She put her fingers to his mouth again. "I love you."

"Are you sure?"

"Yes. A second time, yes."

His mouth and tongue claimed her, invaded her, filled her with joy again. A moment later, though, he set her away. "I have to go, but I've a reason to come back now."

Alarm stopped the ecstasy of a second before. "What do you mean? What are you talking about?"

"It's the kid. The one in the gang. He wants to meet with me, without Luis. He says Luis is planning something, something that has to do with you and Josh and the church."

"You didn't tell me that."

"I couldn't. I—"

"Don't go, Reece. I don't trust him."

"I have to. If I don't…well, we won't know for sure which one we can trust."

"Can't you call the police? Someone? Ask Rich to go with you." Her voice rose, panicked.

"Kati." He removed her hands from his arms, lowering

them gently to her side. "I can't. He won't come near if there's one whiff of a cop. You have to pray. Go home and pray. Trust God."

She fought the tears again, fought the terror. "I...I..."

"God is big enough for this, and if... No, just go home and pray. Get in your car, go home, and pray. I'll call you later."

***

But he hadn't called.

Terror tried to grip her. She pushed it away, reached out to God, prayed as Reece had asked. She quoted Scripture. Aloud. She marched and shook her fist at the devil and claimed Reece's righteousness and safety in Jesus' name. She asked for angels to protect him—as if one couldn't do the deed, as if he needed a legion.

Why was she so afraid?

Lord, what is going on? Are you telling me something?

Two hours passed, and she hadn't heard from him. She marched around her living room one more time, picked up her phone, and stopped.

Should she text him? What if she caused a problem? She'd seen movies where one little jangle from a phone could throw the good guy off. Or it might throw off the bad guy. Or maybe she was just being silly.

After a moment, she texted. *Reece, hi. Please call or text.*

Nothing.

He could be busy.

She waited, walked around her living area again. Prayed. *Come on, Reece. Just text.*

A moment later, her phone jingled. She jumped to the table and grabbed it.

A text from Reece. *I'm home. Come to the house.*

Come to the house? He hadn't asked her back or took her back there since the first time. Joshua's off-limits rule, no doubt. But now?

She hesitated. Maybe Joshua was there. A moment later, she reached for her purse and headed out the door. Jaw clenching followed. Had Reece just forgotten to call her then? Maybe turned off his phone? No, he wouldn't do that. What was up?

Kati stopped her Nissan on the street. Her heart leapt. Both cars were in the drive. She climbed out, strode up the walk, and knocked on the door.

Nothing.

She knocked again.

Still nothing. She rapped harder. This time something moved near the window.

"Yeah, it's me, Reece. Open up."

The lock clicked, and the door jerked inward.

She started. And then a dark figure reached out, grabbed her arm, and dragged her inside. Before she could think or scream, an iron hand gripped her mouth and something sharp cut into her neck.

"If you scream, you are dead. Do you hear me? You are dead."

Chapter 11

Take unto you the whole armour of God, that ye may be able to withstand in the evil day, and having done all, to stand.
(Ephesians 6:13 KJV)

Her heart had stopped, as did her brain and muscle. She knew she should be doing something—extricating herself from his hold or bringing a knee to his groin, but her body iced over.

The knife moved again, and her airway closed.

"Ah, chica linda, just who I was waiting for. Your novios are here. Maybe not as you would expect them." With his arm tight around her, he thrust her toward the back of the house.

The light from the bedroom window cast a surreal glow over the room. Reece lay sprawled facedown on the floor. Her breath ratcheted from her lungs, and she fought the rising wash of blackness.

No, Lord, no. Let him be okay. Alive. Please.

Joshua sat in a chair, hands behind his back. She saw the alarm in his gaze as their eyes met.

"Kati." Josh's voice made no sound, but she saw his lips move, and she knew it was a guttural cry. "What are you doing here?"

"I texted her to come, fundie." His grin was malicious. He nodded toward Reece. "On her man's phone."

He shoved her forward. She stumbled over Reece and fell, her hands and knees slamming the floor. The next instant, she scrambled to Reece's side and grabbed his shoulders. They were warm. Relief flooded her. She tried to turn him over.

"Leave him alone!"

Her head jerked up. Recognition hit—the man—no, the teenager—was the one on the motorcycle the night she and Joshua had been last to leave the church. Certainly he was younger than he appeared then. And Reece had come to meet him. What happened?

Lord, please help.

"Get the tape from the floor next to the pastor." The teen indicated the duct tape near Joshua. When she hesitated, he pulled a gun from the waistband of his jeans and pointed it at Reece. "If he comes to before you tape him up, he dies."

"What do you want?" Joshua's voice, tight but calm, cut across the teen's words.

Kati scooted next to Joshua and grabbed the tape. Her eyes landed on the red stain on the side of his shirt, and her eyes flew up to meet his, but he kept his gaze on the kid.

"Get the tape and tape your boyfriend's hands and ankles." The teen thrust her away from Joshua. "Do it!"

As she scrambled back to Reece, her brain began to function. What had happened to Joshua? How long had Reece been out? Why was he out? A wet spot in Reece's hair looked dark, as if it could be blood. Had the man hit him with something?

"Tie his ankles."

Kati unpeeled the tape. Would she be able to do this loose? Would that make any difference with duct tape? She wound it twice around his ankles, then stopped. She had nothing to cut it with. She looked at the teen and indicated the tape.

"Get back." He pointed with his chin to where she should move. The gun went back into the waistband of his jeans. He stepped forward and ripped the tape with his knife. "Do his wrists."

As she moved forward again, Reece groaned. Her eyes jerked to the teen. He shifted the knife and pulled the gun.

"No!" Joshua shouted.

Kati threw herself forward and covered Reece's body with her own.

"You'd better tie him up, puta. Quickly."

Out of the corner of her eye, Kati saw Joshua wince. She grabbed the tape and leaned forward just as Reece started to roll over.

"Tie him now!"

She grabbed one of Reece's hands, but he pulled free. "Don't move, Reece. Don't move." She thought an eye opened, but he groaned, rolled onto his back, and lay still. She grabbed his other hand, pulled both together, and circled the tape around his wrists.

She looked at the teen again. The hatred in his eyes shook her. What had they ever done to elicit that?

"Get back. Get away from him."

She scooted a foot or two back across the floor.

The teen pulled out a phone and sent a text.

Under her breath, Kati began to pray. "Lord, help us. Please send someone or set us free—somehow."

"I asked what you wanted," Joshua said. "If there's something we could do—"

"Shut up! You shut up." He waved the gun then looked at Kati. "I told you to get back."

She moved back another foot, drew her feet in.

Joshua shifted. "You know, Luis told us we'd be safe here. Isn't he your leader, your capitán?

"Luis does not always control, but you have no worry. Luis will be here to see this." His gaze ran over Kati. "And maybe to have some fun with the señorita."

Kati sucked in her breath, shuddered. The teen stuck the gun back into his pants and pulled the knife again. He eyed Reece, but Reece had not moved. The kid waited a moment, then leaned over to cut the tape from the roll.

Reece's taped hands shot up, connecting hard with the

teen's chin. A yell ripped from the boy's mouth, and he stumbled backward. Kati shot to her feet even as Reece rolled forward and swung his hands at the boy's shins. The teen staggered, then lunged downward with the knife.

Blood gushed in a red line across Reece's arm. As the boy's hand came up again, Kati lurched forward and threw a punch. It barely grazed him.

His head jumped up, and he lunged across Reece, knife raised. Kati sidestepped, launched a front kick, and hurled him against the wall. He slid to the floor. The knife clattered free. He groaned but didn't move.

She stared, heart thumping, and then she vaulted over Reece and grabbed at the gun in his waistband. Reece's warning shout came as the teen seized her wrist. She twisted free and sent a jab to his jaw. His head flew back and slammed against the wall.

She stepped back, gulping air, watching him warily.

"Do it, Kati. Get the gun." Reece's voice leapt at her, rough and insistent.

She leaned over and wrestled the gun free, then backed up and almost fell over Reece. He flinched.

"Careful. Put the gun down near Josh and get the knife. Cut us free. Hurry."

"What about your arm?" Blood oozed across it, dripped to the floor.

"In a minute. Cut Josh free. Quick."

Kati snatched up the knife and ran to Josh. She put the gun down and sawed through the tape.

"Hurry, Kate." Joshua's voice held the same edge as Reece's had.

She whirled at movement behind her. Reece pulled his legs up, then lifted his hands above his head and yanked downward. The tape around his wrists ripped, split. She stared. He'd broken the duct tape.

He looked her way. "Give me the knife. Quick."

The teen moaned and began to pull his feet under him.

Joshua stood. "I'm free."

"Good. Grab the gun. Kati, the knife." Reece's voice was urgent. "Hurry."

Something moved in the doorway. Kati jerked around. Her heart stuttered.

Luis stood in the doorway. "No one moves." His eyes narrowed as they flicked to the teen and back to them. The gun in his hand looked bigger and more deadly than the one she'd put on the nightstand.

The kid pushed himself to his feet, put a hand to his jaw, and glared at Kati before spewing forth a rush of Spanish words.

Luis jerked his head between the two and said something. A question. The teen answered between gritted teeth. Luis' eyes came back to Kati, contemplative. Was that the briefest flash of amusement in the man's face before he stepped back and glanced down at Reece? His focus moved from the tape around Reece's ankles, to the broken tape, to the bloody arm. A fraction of a second later, his eyes and the gun were on Joshua.

"Don't move, Pastor. The gun is quicker than you are. And your friend here needs someone to attend to that wound. Don't distract me."

"I...I can do it," Kati said.

The kid stepped forward. "No. I tell you, Luis, you can't trust her."

"Shut up, Mateo. You told me something was going on, texted me to come here." The dark eyes sent a warning look to the teen. "Now it seems I need to clean up your mess."

A movement from Reece brought the gun's aim to Kati. "Your attempt to get to me, hombre, will result in this one's death." He stepped back and gave a jerk with his head to the teen. Mateo moved back also.

Kati swallowed, her spine rigid, her muscles tight as tent cords.

"Now, chica, fix up your man here. Do it quickly."

Kati hesitated. The man frowned and gave another jerk with his head, and Kati dropped beside Reece, then looked around. "I need the pillowcase from the bed."

The man's eyes narrowed, but he gave a nod of assent. She grabbed the pillow, pulled the case off, and bent next to Reece, wiped his arm as clean as possible. The blood still flowed, but had slowed. *Thank you, Lord.* She needed something to make a bandage.

"Use the tape, Kati. Just tape the skin together." Reece's voice still sounded rough.

She looked into his eyes. They were steady, serious. She snatched the tape and wrapped it around his arm, covering the wound, making sure it wasn't too tight. When she looked for the knife, Mateo spat another line of Spanish at Luis.

"Tear it," Luis said.

Her fingers trembled, but she did, leaning over and biting it and tearing it down.

"Kati." Reese's voice barely reached her. "I'm going to roll his way. You need to—"

"I'm trying to keep you alive, hombre, but you're about to snap my good intención." Luis' voice held a dangerous edge. "Back up, chica. Against the wall."

Mateo flung other words after her. His leer made her cringe.

Joshua straightened, the line across his jaw tightening. Kati glanced his way. His eyes caught hers, then swung back to the gang leader.

"Luis." Joshua's voice was firm, solid. "I was telling…Mateo…whatever he's afraid of, whatever hurts inside, God can take care of that. He can give you a new life. You can step away from this life and find another."

The gang leader's eyebrow rose. Now definite amusement showed. "You preaching to us, Pastor? We're holding a gun on you, and you're preaching to us?"

Joshua met his look. "You could kill us, and we'd be standing at the gates of heaven the next instant. Where would you be?"

Mateo's face darkened. "They act like they have no fear." He moved and picked up his knife from the floor. "I could teach them fear."

Luis' head shot around. Spanish spewed from his mouth, eyes narrowed to slits now.

Mateo backed up a step, but he straightened, spitting forth words of his own, moving the knife threateningly.

Luis slammed his gun across the teen's face and sent him flying. Kati gasped. Joshua moved as if to step forward, then stopped.

Luis glared at Mateo. "Estúpido. You want the whole police force down on us? They're amigos with that detective."

The teen edged closer to Luis. "They won't know what happened to them. We can make them disappear. And you can have the girl. I brought her here for you. I give her to you."

Luis spat on the floor. "If I wanted the girl, I would have her."

Mateo dropped his eyes. "Sí, sí. I only meant…"

Luis stuck the gun in Mateo's side. The younger man's eyes widened.

"Cut the hombre free."

Mateo's nose flared, and his eyes went cold. He used the knife to point at Reece. "This one disrespected you. He deserves to pay."

Luis grabbed the front of his shirt. "Disrespected? He had a gun that day. You didn't even know. You missed it. He respected me by getting his gun, made me from the house, and knew he might need it. Idiota!" He shoved him away.

Mateo spun around and brought the knife up. "You're losing it, man. You're allowing them to walk through our neighborhood. They're making us, man. Watching us."

"And what will they see? *Nada. Nothing.*" Luis shoved his

165

face into Mateo's. "Unless we want them to. You gonna blow these three? You'll bring a heat wave down on us like we've never had. Get over there and cut him free. I'll get you out of this."

Mateo hesitated. "He can make me from the fire."

"¿De qué hablas?"

"The fire. He saw me."

"The gym fire? You did that?" Luis' face was in his. "You take it on yourself to do this?"

"I…I was getting money for us."

"And where's the money?"

"He wouldn't pay. That's why I light the fire."

"Estas loco! If you weren't my sister's hermanito, I'd drill you right here." Luis' face was so close to Mateo's that spittle landed on the other's face.

Mateo pulled back. The look of fear gave way to anger. His eyes changed; hatred jumped through them. His arm shot forward. The knife buried itself into Luis' gut. Luis' eyes rounded. He grabbed the hilt of the knife, stumbled back, and dropped to the floor. The gun flew from his hand.

Kati screamed.

Reece lunged for the gun, but his taped ankles brought him up short. He hit the floor and rolled. Mateo scrambled after the gun. The teen's fingers closed over it just as Joshua crashed into him. Both went down. Joshua jumped on top of him. The teen tried to throw him off, but Joshua slammed him with his fist. When he did, the kid dropped the gun, reached up, and grabbed Joshua around the waist. Next instant, he'd pulled Joshua forward and down. The teen exploded upward, rocked Joshua sideways, then scrambled on top. He rained down punches over Joshua's face.

Kati leapt forward and sent a kick to the teen's side. His head jerked around. She kicked him again, and he curled himself into a ball. A moment later he rolled off Josh, snatching at the gun and springing to his feet.

As the gun swung her way, Kati stopped short and yanked her arms up. Her breath caught, and her heart slammed like a tidal wave. Reece had risen again to a sitting position, tearing at the tape on his ankles, but froze.

Words spewed at them, and the gun wove back and forth.

"In Jesus' name…" Joshua's voice rose in a ragged plea.

Mateo spun toward him. The words spewing from him sounded vile and guttural. The gun wove back and forth.

Joshua sprawled next to Luis, blood flowing from his mouth and nose. His eyes fixated on the gun, but he slowly pushed himself to a sitting position.

The gun jerked his way, and the teen's breath rasped. "Do not try anything. I will kill all of you, even the girl."

On the floor, near him, Luis moved, groaned.

Mateo's eyes, cold and hard, dropped to the gang leader. "Maybe we have a new capitán, *brother*," Mateo ground out.

Kati shivered.

Luis half rose, spitting Spanish words at him, the violence in his voice unmistakable.

Mateo's eyes narrowed, and a malevolent expression dropped over his face. He swung the gun and ground out three words.

"No!" Joshua yelled and threw himself in front of Luis. The gun exploded, Joshua jerked once, and he fell back against Luis. Both men tumbled to the ground. Neither moved.

Reece's bellow followed. He ripped the tape from his ankles even as Mateo staggered from the big gun's recoil. Reece launched himself at the teen.

"Joshua!" Kati screamed and ran forward. "Joshua!" No response. Her throat tightened. She grabbed his shoulder.

Sounds to her left jerked her head up. Reece had his hand around Mateo's wrist even as Joshua had earlier. She saw his hand whiten with the pressure.

"Drop it." Reece's voice sounded deadly. He lifted the teen's hand and pounded it against the floor. When Mateo squirmed and threw a left-handed punch, Reece reared back and brought a right cross to his face. The kid's head rolled, and the gun dropped to the floor.

Kati stared. Would the teen get free again? He seemed almost possessed. Coming back each time—against all three of them.

Jesus, help us.

Reece snatched up the gun and pushed himself off the kid. He stood, stepped back, and trained the gun on him, but Mateo didn't move.

Kati dropped her gaze and rolled Joshua off Luis. His head moved; his mouth drew sideways.

"Josh." Her voice was a plea. The red stain on the front of his shirt fanned out like a huge amoeba.

Lord…

Her brain computed the wound, her mind adding together what she saw even as it echoed with denial. She looked frantically for the pillowcase to staunch the bleeding.

Joshua's eyes opened. He grasped her wrist. "Help…Reece."

She looked up, wondering what he meant. Reece's head snapped her way, eyes wide. He stepped away from the teen.

Luis groaned and struggled to sit up.

"Stay there!" Kati ordered. The man's blood covered the front of his shirt too, the knife still buried but to the side. "Stay still!" The knife had not been large, but if the gang leader wasn't careful, he would bleed out. She glanced down at Joshua. They'd both bleed out.

They needed an ambulance. *Now.*

Joshua's face had paled. Its ashen color caused her heart to lurch.

His mouth stretched, moved. She leaned closer.

"Help him stand, Kate. Help him."

"Josh…"

"He needs you." His head dropped to the side.

"Josh, hang on!"

He drew an unsteady breath. "I'm going home, Kate." The soft squeeze of his hand against her wrist, and a smile, and then his eyes closed.

"Joshua!"

Reece jerked at her voice and took a step toward them, his eyes filled with shocked denial.

Mateo stirred, and Reece twisted back, the gun in his hand rising. His face hardened. "If you want to live, gamberro, don't move." His eyes narrowed on the kid. "Kati, find a phone. Call 911."

Chapter 12

But God who is rich in mercy, for his great love wherewith he loved us.
(Ephesians 2:4 KJV)

Reece paced the small office, his heart as heavy as an anvil. How had Josh prepared anything here? His eyes clenched together. He swallowed. *What do you want me to do, buddy? I'm not you.*

He'd been back over that day a dozen times. Could he have done something different? Should he have taken Kati's advice and not gone? No. Mateo would have found another way.

The kid had surprised him by being in the house when he got home, but he could have turned it around if he hadn't pulled his punch when he saw how young Mateo was. Sixteen, seventeen at the most. The times he'd seen him before—at the gym, in the street—had been far enough away not to show the baby face, and Reece had pulled his punch at the shock of it.

But Mateo, young or not, was a street fighter. The boy was as tall as Josh and strong. He'd taken advantage of Reece's hesitation. They'd struggled and landed on the floor. The scuffle had alerted the teen to Reece's SOB holster and the gun. Wrestling with a gun in a small-of-the-back holster was painful and dangerous. When he'd hit the wall trying to keep the kid's knife from his gut, the Glock had slammed into his back, ricocheting pain through his body. And he'd underestimated the teen's ability. Those mistakes could have proved fatal, would have with an opponent more experienced, because Reece had been out of the fight scene for three years.

When he'd thrown a punch to get off the wall, the kid had blocked it with an open hand and used his other hand to hit Reece's bicep and smack the side of his face at eye level. Kung fu moves. Yeah, he'd underestimated him. Then the teen had wrapped his arms around Reece, going for the gun, and he'd come up with it. Reece knew he should be dead, but it was Mateo's turn to hesitate. The realization hit him that Mateo wasn't used to a gun. The teen's weapon of choice—the knife—was on the floor, and Reece had installed a thumb safety on his own weapon. It gave Reece one more chance, one he desperately needed—except, a car had pulled into the driveway.

They'd both heard it, and Reece knew who it was. Joshua coming home way too early. He'd rushed the teen, and the kid had pulled the trigger. Or tried. The safety worked. They both went down as Reece hit him, the gun flying across the room. Somehow the kid had grabbed the knife from the floor, and as Joshua came in, Mateo scrambled to his feet, caught Josh around the neck, and shoved the knife into his side.

It had stopped Reece in his tracks. Things had gone downhill from there. Holding Joshua hostage, Mateo had retrieved the gun. The kid wasn't stupid. One glance down had shown him the safety, and he'd flicked it off. Then he'd forced them to the back bedroom, where he'd ordered Reece to tape Joshua to the chair.

The teen had done lots of talking after Josh had walked into the ambush—of how he would be demanding protection money from all the businesses around there, even the churches. He'd texted and called Luis a number of times, and finally got a response. From what Reece could make out, Mateo never told Luis what was going down. He was a kid still, wanting to show off. Reece's stomach had churned at that. A sixteen-year-old that might kill them just to show off.

But Mateo hadn't known what to do with Reece once Josh was taped to the chair. He knew enough not to get too close. Threats to kill Joshua if Reece tried anything followed, and Reece had to respect those. The stalemate would have broken somehow, if Kati hadn't pounded on the door and called his name. His heart had dropped then, past his feet into the ground.

The teen had grinned as if expecting her and held up Reece's phone. When had he gotten it? During the scuffle? Or afterward, when he'd seen it lying on the floor, perhaps? It didn't matter now. Reece hadn't realized it was gone. So, all the texts the boy had sent had not gone to Luis.

A threat to kill her ensured that Reece turned his back to the teen as ordered. Every nerve ending in his body roared. He thought he would die then, but Mateo had only slammed the gun down across his head. He'd gone down but never completely out.

Remembering it now, Reece closed his eyes and dropped onto the chair across the desk from Joshua's. He wouldn't sit in Josh's chair. He put his head in his hands. *What happened, Lord? How do I make sense of this? Wasn't this why you had me here? To make sure this didn't happen?* Guilt threatened to strangle him, as it had for the last week.

Could he have done something differently? If he'd gotten free sooner, if he'd gone for *his* gun instead of Luis' that first time, if he hadn't underestimated the kid, if…if…

None of it would bring Joshua back. None of it. His throat worked. He had to bring something to these people that would honor his friend, something that would make Josh proud…

Their last conversation came back. Joshua forcing him to listen, more earnest than he'd ever seen him. "You, Reece Jernigan, have a calling from God. You know it. I know it. You're not here to protect me. I know where you're coming from, but if God doesn't protect me, you can't either. Stop running from your *real* calling. Now. We haven't any more time. Surrender to it. And stop making me the scapegoat. I'm no holier than you are. Quit that stuff. You're adored by the Father. He loves you—as much as He loves me or Kati or anyone else. You told Kati she was a warrior. Well, *you're a warrior*. It's time to step up to the fight. Pick up your sword and shut up the Enemy!"

He heaved a sigh, swallowed again. He hadn't been able to save him, and God hadn't protected him. But why? Had the Enemy won? Reece didn't believe that. Even when things happened that he didn't understand, he knew ultimately God would have his way, would bring something good out of it.

His heart still felt like an anvil in his chest. It had been easy to be in Josh's shadow. Now what would he do? How could he prepare for his friend's funeral? He wouldn't be able to speak. He sent a look upward. And Pastor Alan still couldn't make it back. *What is that, Lord? What are you doing to me?*

Unless…unless he challenged everyone at the funeral with the words Josh had challenged him with. A swift jolt of amusement went through him. It would be using Joshua one last time, using his friend's words. And Joshua would be laughing, telling all the angels that he'd get Reece yet. He nodded. He could see that. He could do that. Challenge them to the fight. Gladiators, warriors, soldiers. They were in the army. Not all would survive this world, but all would celebrate in the one to come.

Chapter 13

Stand therefore, having girded your waist with truth, having put on the breastplate of righteousness, and having shod your feet with the preparation of the gospel of peace; above all, taking the shield of faith with which you will be able to quench all the fiery darts of the wicked one. And take the helmet of salvation, and the sword of the Spirit, which is the word of God; praying always with all prayer and supplication in the Spirit, being watchful to this end with all perseverance and supplication for all the saints.
(Ephesians 6:14–18 NKJV)

Reece stood in front of the pulpit, hands sweating, jaw clenched. The sanctuary had filled to capacity. Many he didn't recognize. His fervent wish was that they could have cut off all those who hadn't known Josh, but then Josh's family wouldn't have seen how his sacrifice had ignited the community. They wouldn't know how, in such a short time, God had used him to pour out his love to many, used him to call others to stand in the gap, to fight, to exit their comfort zones, and to love.

Tears caught in his throat as he looked at Josh's mom and dad, his sister, and his grandmother. He'd shed tears with them already. He and Kati and the others. *Lord, only you will get me through this.*

He bowed his head as the music weaved its way into his soul. Words about God's faithfulness, his strength and his unfailing love. The music ended; the whispering stopped. He raised his head, eyes finding Kati, who had commandeered his own grandmother when she arrived, unannounced, from out of town. The ghost of a smile started inside. His *nain* would always be there for him, as Josh had been, even when she went home to heaven.

He raised his eyes toward the ceiling. Even as Josh *was*. He felt his friend's compassion and amusement, heard his voice. "Step up, bro. The people won't wait all day."

Reece smiled then and let his eyes flicker over the room. He cleared this throat. "Josh would have loved that you are all here today. He would have preached his heart out, explained the grace and love of Jesus to you even as he did to me over the last three years, and ask anyone that didn't know him to reach out to him. Until you know Jesus, you know so little of the world, of life, and of love.

"Joshua's life showed Jesus. You couldn't really understand that until you'd been on the streets with him, watched him walk up to gang members and share Jesus with them. I mean, here I am reaching for my Glock, and here he was reaching for a hug."

Laughter rolled across the sanctuary. Reece looked around again. "Now if you're in a gang, or were—I see some faces from my old neighborhood—thank you for being here. Joshua would have loved seeing you all sitting there." He swallowed, pushed back the tears. "You know I'm not insulting you. A Glock could be an important part of your colors some days.

"Josh was all about the other guy, the same way Jesus is. I don't know how many times he was in my face about God's love and grace and mercy. He didn't give up, didn't quit. Neither does Jesus. Josh sacrificed his life for someone else's. Jesus did, too. He sacrificed his life for *you*.

"Sin is a killer. Are you hurting today? Feeling broken? Or just overwhelmed by life and what it has done to you? That's where I was. Jesus can change that. I know. I had terrorized people." He stopped and closed his eyes for a moment. "But God forgives, cleanses, makes whole. From the ashes of my life, he brought something new, something different. My own gang tried to kill me when I received Jesus. Then they tried to kill Josh. God rescued us, miraculously, and the gang backed off. They said we had angels protecting us. I think we did."

Pain shot through him. *Why didn't you save him again, Lord? Why?* Reece slid another glance upward.

"Why didn't God save him again? I have no answers. I only know that in a war, not all survive, not all come out unscathed. We get some things messed up. As Christians, we think nothing should happen to us here on earth. After all, we know Christ. We know his power. Or at least know of it. But we forget, while we are in these suits"—Reece hit his chest—"we are in a battle. We can ignore it, go the way of the world, fill our lives with feel-good stuff or…we can take the place that God has called us to and join the battle. This was where Josh was. In the battle.

"I'm not saying you all have to be on the streets. Your war might be taking food to a neighbor or praying for a small boy because his mother asked." He smiled at Kati.

She bit her lip. Tears slid down her face.

"It's up to God to direct you. Not me. Not anyone but God.

"I'm not a great speaker. I don't have words like Josh did, and I'm going to ask his family and friends to come up here and give us some insights into Josh's life, but before I step down, I just want to say one more thing. Don't let Joshua's sacrifice be for nothing. Don't let Jesus' sacrifice be for nothing. A God who loves you unconditionally, who accepts you just as you are, is waiting for you. Step out of your comfort zone and away from your fear, and step into the abundant life awaiting you."

He nodded at China, who moved to the front row. She took an older woman by the arm to help her to the platform. Reece went down the other stairs to sit by Kati and his grandmother.

Fights in his old neighborhood had nothing to compare with what the next hour would bring. His heart was already scarred.

When everyone who wanted to share about Joshua had stepped down, Reece moved back to the pulpit. Tears and laughter had touched him through the sharing.

"When you think about Joshua, remember his greatest desire is to see you in Christ. If you want to talk with me later, please call the church office, and China will get in touch with me." His gaze passed over the crowd and rested momentarily on a person in the back. "Let's pray."

A minute later, people stood and chatted or headed out the back door. Reece walked down the platform stairs. Kati stepped forward. He kept his eyes on the back door. "Kati, I have to reach someone. Can you take my grandmother back to her motel? Tell her I'll be there later."

He moved around others crowding his way and tried his best not to offend as he pushed forward. He muttered excuses as he passed people wanting to talk with him. He thrust the back doors open and trotted down the steps.

"Luis."

The gang leader stiffened and turned. His hand rested on the handlebars of the motorcycle.

Reece walked slowly his way. "¿Como estas? You're out of the hospital already?"

Luis' hand started toward his stomach, stopped. "Mateo has no strength of hand, only thickness of brain. The wound was not as serious as it looked. The doctors were amazed that I walk out of the hospital the next day."

"Good." Reece nodded. "A miracle, maybe?" When the gang leader's face showed puzzlement, Reece merely smiled. "Josh would have been glad to hear that and glad you came."

"He took a dive for me. I came." His eyes flicked over Reece. "I don't understand why the man would do that. Throw himself in front of me."

"That was Josh. And that's Jesus."

"I don't get religion, man."

"Neither do I, but I get relationship and understanding that someone loves me."

Luis' mouth clenched, and he turned toward the motorcycle.

"You know, I'm talking about the God of the universe, the God who made everything. Not just some made-up squirrelly thing, but a real God. Who loves you. Who has a purpose for your life. He saved you for a reason."

"I'm too far gone, man. No one, no god gonna love me."

"You're never too far gone for Jesus. His love encompasses us all."

Luis shook his head and eyed Reece. "What's your story?"

"The Dogs. Welsh gang. New York."

"Yeah." He nodded. "I thought so. Mateo was stupid. Had no idea you could be dangerous. He wouldn't have survived much longer. Snitches were already telling me his stuff." He swung his leg over the bike. "He wanted to take over since the moment I let him into the gang."

"Your sister's brother? Not yours?"

"A different dad. Mateo was always different, too. Impatient, mean."

"You can get out. I did."

"The gang is all I have. It's all I know."

"That can change. You'd have help here." Even as he said it, he wondered what they'd do if Luis wanted help now. They would need extra buildings for digs, counselors, Bible teachers, job placement people, and more. And the church, the people of God, would have to back it, have to give of their time and their finances. If God wanted what Reece thought he wanted, they'd all have to give a lot. The weight inside him moved, lightened a little. Because of Josh's sacrifice, many would do just that.

Luis started his motorcycle, shook his head. "Leave the gang? This would happen." He moved a finger across his throat, but then waved at the church behind Reece. "My sister come here. You keep her safe. Her husband's away, and some hombres have tried to move in on her."

"You should be there for her, Luis."

Luis glowered. He waved again at the church. "You."

"I'll check on her and have Kati stop by. But you—"

Luis' face lightened. "Your woman? You let her out of your sight?"

"To see your sister." Reece couldn't help the growl in his voice. He still didn't like Luis' interest in Kati.

Luis laughed before his face settled into a quizzical expression. "You defend me with the police."

"You weren't the problem. Mateo was." Something curled inside his stomach at the kid's name, something repulsive, yet with the touch of healing in it. Like warm milk. It would be the hardest thing he'd ever done, but he'd have to go see Mateo in jail, and he'd have to forgive him… Forgiveness was vital if he wanted the ministry to work. The seed of bitterness would ruin it. He just wasn't there yet. He brought his focus back to Luis. But he would get there. God would get him there.

The man nodded, studied Reece another moment, then roared out of the parking lot.

There, Father, goes a man you love. Help me to reach him.

He took a deep breath, squared his shoulders, and turned back to the people who waited for him.

***

It was two days after the funeral, and Reece wondered where she was. They hadn't talked since his message, since Josh's body was lowered into the grave, since their gazes had met before Reece was surrounded by family and friends. He wanted to find her, to hold her, talk with her. So much to say. And yet…

He didn't want to do it until he'd had his talk with God, but he'd put it off.

The house was empty. Too empty. The pain still too close to the surface. That was why he needed her, wanted her. Just sharing it, sharing their love for Joshua would help. Sharing the laughter, too.

He stared out the front window. A hummingbird flitted around the feeder. Zipped in, zipped out. God of angel armies. And flesh ones, too. Why did hummers always make him think of angels? Crazy. Because from what he could understand, angels looked like gladiators and made men drop to their knees.

His gaze followed the hummer's flight. It stopped, wings whipping back and forth, hovering, looking at him through the window. Then it darted forward. Dread hit him instantly. No way did he want to see this tiny thing smashed onto his window. But the bird stopped short, cocked its head at Reece, and darted away.

Wait! It was almost out his mouth. His head and hand followed the bird, and his fingers hit the window pane.

"Ow!" He yanked his hand back, shook it, and turned, expecting Joshua to be there, expecting his laugh.

Realization hit him harder than at any time before. He dropped to his knees, crying out. "What did you do, Josh? What crazy thing did you do? You're supposed to be here."

Tears flooded his eyes, and this time he didn't stifle them. He let them come.

Later, a long time later, he looked up, stared up, and said brokenly, "What did *you* do? Why did you let this happen?" In the silence, without words, was the knowing, the knowing that God was doing something. He didn't have to reason about Joshua. He only had to know that God was still God, and he would get Reece through this.

Josh was my anchor, Jesus. I know it's supposed to be you, but he was it. I could see you behind and around him, and that was all I thought I needed. Paul said follow me as I follow Christ. Why couldn't I just follow Josh? The silence intensified. The knowing moved again across his heart, not even needing his mind. *Help me, Father. I need you now more than ever. I need to know what I'm to do, where I'm to go. Enable me to do whatever it is you're calling me to. Let me to see your power. I want your will in my life and my relationships. If Kati belongs with me, let me know. Let us both know. Give me the grace and courage to follow your leading. May your desires become mine.*

He stopped, took a breath. "Let Joshua be proud of me." He stopped again. "Let Jesus be proud of me."

***

Kati stood on the back deck. The hummers zipped and spun and chased each other. She wanted to laugh, but her chest heaved. She wanted to cry, too. Reece hadn't called or come by since the funeral, and she needed him. Wanted him.

What is he doing, Lord? She slipped into one of the chairs near the table. *I have to stop feeling sorry for myself. If he wants to come, he will. He's going through enough right now.* She lifted her head. *Lord, you've called him, haven't you?* The words he'd said at the funeral were said to himself as well as to all those who attended. How many people Joshua had touched in the short time he'd been here. Funny that Pastor Alan couldn't make it back for the funeral. Funny that Reece had to do it.

Funnier still that Daneen had called to inquire about how he was and then went on to say they were thinking about asking Reece to take over the assistant pastor's position. That Pastor Alan felt God wanted to continue what Joshua had started and to enlarge it. More prayer walks, a food and clothing ministry, one-on-one evangelism, and perhaps a house for those trying to get out of the gangs or free from drugs.

"We don't see it all now, but we think Reece will. He knows what people need in these circumstances. We're looking at something bigger than we've ever been involved in, but…well, we think God is calling us this way. The Scriptures tell us to go out into the highways and the byways and compel them to come in—to the wedding! A celebration! And for that we are all going to need grace, and Reece knows grace. Joshua said Reece is all about grace."

The heat from the sun beat into her face. Would Reece even want to do this? Would he compare himself to Joshua?

"Lord, that wouldn't be fair. If you're calling him, let him know you want him to be himself, not someone else. And I love him. What am I supposed to do with that, Lord? Are we supposed to be together? Let him know, Lord. Please."

"Who are you talking to?" Reece's voice jumped at her.

She shot up from the chair and whirled around. "Reece!"

He came from the side of the house and up the steps to the deck, his look a little sheepish. "Were you talking about me?"

"I…I…"

He stepped in front of her, blocked the sun from her eyes. "You love me?"

"I told you before."

"But it's good to know for sure."

"Is it?"

He nodded slowly, and then his mouth curved upward. "Yeah. Saves me a lot of beating around the bush. I love you, too. Want to get married?"

"What?" Her breath hitched. "Is that a proposal?"

He touched her cheek, his smile broadening. "Sounded like one to me."

"No getting on one knee, no skywriter, no ring?"

"No skywriter? Is that what you want? I can do that. But I'd thought of something different. Something that included a ring. It was going to be a surprise, but…"

"No, no, don't tell me!"

"So does that mean when I get the ring and do the surprise, the answer will be yes?"

"Are you always this romantic? Is this what I can expect?"

"Come here." He drew her into his arms.

The kiss began with soft gentleness, brushing his lips against hers, but then he tightened his hold and increased the pressure of his mouth. It sent waves of warmth through her.

He moved his lips to her ear. "You can expect more of this."

She pulled her head back. "You sure you haven't had too much to drink, sir?"

He drew away and slapped his chest. "You do me a dishonor, maiden. My love is from the purest heart. Well, as pure as God can make it."

"God can make it as white as snow, and yours is."

"That's why I love you, Kate. You see us all through Christ's blood."

She stilled. "You called me Kate."

"I know." His brows lowered. The dark eyes deepened with sadness. "I know it was Joshua's name for you. Mind if I use it once in a while?"

Her heart squeezed at his tone. She touched his hand. "No, I don't mind. We'll keep him alive here, won't we? You can tell me things I never knew about him."

He nodded, his smile like sunlight forcing its way through charcoal clouds.

"I love you, Reece. I loved Joshua, too. Just not in the same way."

The light through his smile shone brighter, and he closed her in his arms.

***

Reece almost ignored the knock on the door, but he struggled up from the chair, stopping for a moment to glance out the front window. The man standing there didn't look like he belonged to the neighborhood. Casual but well dressed. In his midforties, maybe. A Jeep was parked on the street out front. *A Jeep.*

Only a week since Joshua's death. Reece wasn't up for social calls. He heaved a sigh and pulled the door open.

"Reece Jernigan?" When Reece nodded, the man's eyes filled with compassion. "I'm Pastor Alan. You cannot know how sorry I am that I wasn't here these last few weeks."

Weeks? Was it only weeks? Reece steadied his heart and waved the pastor in.

The man stepped into the house, glanced around, then settled his gaze on Reece. "Joshua told me so much about you that I feel we should know each other."

"You barely knew him." Reece couldn't stop the hardness of his voice.

"You're right. Not in the way you mean. But he and I talked over the phone. Texted. Emailed. A lot. He loved God, he loved you, and he loved the vision God had put on him."

Reece grunted.

"I've been in the county jail once. That was enough for me. Never made it into prison. Kept to drinking and weed and petty theft when growing up. I may not know as much about the people in this neighborhood as you do, but I have been in places where they have. The vision that God gave Joshua about this area coincided with what God gave me."

"Coincided?" The man sounded like Joshua. *Coincided.* He couldn't help the smirk.

"Yeah. God put that same desire in me. Right now you might not feel you can go on without him, and I felt for a short time that the Enemy had snatched away the vision. But we both know that the gifts and callings of God are without repentance, without change. He's called you here, and he's called me. I'm not giving up, and I hope you're not giving up either. Together we can see the vision God gave for this neighborhood fulfilled. These people are worth more than us buckling right now. They need you. I need you."

Reece stared. The fear of man was nothing like the fear of God calling you to do something when you knew you had no ability to do it.

Pastor Alan waved his hand. "You may not want this right now, but I wouldn't be here if I didn't feel God told me to come and told me to *compel* you to come in." He grinned suddenly, his face looking ten years younger. "Don't you love a challenge? Here's one for you. Help fulfill the vision God gave Joshua. He now gives it to us."

Reece still didn't say a word, didn't know if he could. Skydiving never scared him as much as the thought of going on without Joshua.

"You need time to grieve and heal, Reece. I'm not insensitive to your pain, your loss. But I want to offer whatever help I can. We don't know each other, but we will. Come to the church tomorrow or the next day, and let's talk about whatever's on your heart. If not, then I heard skydiving is a great release of tension."

The pastor grinned again, and Reece knew Josh had told him about that first terrifying experience of jumping from the plane. Josh always did things that terrified him—like walking into the worst neighborhood in Manhattan and preaching to the gangs there. Reece felt the smile start on his face, and the other man's eyes lit. He held out his hand, and Reece shook it.

"Pray about this. I hear you have a good woman to help you, too."

When Reece lifted a brow, the pastor laughed. "Joshua told me. He thought you and Kati would make a great team."

"Joshua…" Reece's voice came out in guttural surprise.

"Yeah. He said he loved you both and would be glad to see you together." He backed toward the door. "A day or two?" When Reece nodded, Pastor Alan slipped through the door and walked to the street.

Reece watched the Jeep drive away, his heart thumping to a new and erratic beat, one that was both fearsome and exciting.

Chapter 14

Yea, though I walk through the valley of the shadow of death, I will fear no evil: for thou art with me; thy rod and thy staff they comfort me. Thou preparest a table before me in the presence of mine enemies: thou anointest my head with oil; my cup runneth over. Surely goodness and mercy shall follow me all the days of my life: and I will dwell in the house of the LORD forever.
(Psalm 23:4–6 KJV)

The wind screamed by Kati's ears. Her hair and clothing whipped against her. Fear mixed with the exhilaration of the spin and speed of the fall. She opened her eyes to see the greens and browns and deeper blues hurtle up at them, and she promptly snapped her eyes shut once more. The wind roared past, but the pressure on her back reassured her.

Reece's face snuggled into the corner of her neck. He tapped her shoulder, and she forced her arms out. Her mind stuttered and began to function again. A glittering turquoise sky surrounded her. She was flying! Flying!

Sort of.

They were jumping tandem, and Reece spun them in a circle. Her heart lurched, but as they slowed, she forced her eyes open. Seconds later, Reece tapped her again, and the parachute yanked them upward. The harness mauled her body, and Reece's laughter echoed in her ears. Her fingers dug into the straps around her arms, holding tight. She could see the ground, the buildings, and the cars below them. Clouds billowed on either side, brilliant white against the azure sky.

"You okay?" Reece yelled.

She could feel his body behind hers. She swallowed and nodded.

"I knew you could do this."

"I hoped."

"Adventure is in you."

Had she heard him right? *Adventure in her?*

"Are you ready for the adventure at church?"

Could they just concentrate on getting down? Safely? But she took a deep breath. "If I can do this," she shouted back, "I'm ready."

"Have I told you today that I love you?" Reece bellowed.

"No." The wind snatched her words, and she wasn't sure he'd heard them.

"Well, I do."

"I love you, too."

She took in the sky again. Smiled. All she wanted was to be on the ground. But if he had faith in her, and she had faith in Christ, she could do more than she thought.

Below them, the landing field drew close. People ran along the ground. Red and fuchsia streamers trailed behind them. Strange. Reece reminded her to keep her feet up and out of the way as they landed. Then Reece's feet hit, and they slid across the ground, and relief surged through her.

He unhooked his harness from hers and spun her around. "Did you love it?"

She laughed. "I'm not sure."

"Do you love me?"

"Yes! I'm sure of that!"

"Good." He dug a small box from his jeans and popped it open.

A gold engagement ring with a large square diamond sat in black velvet. Tiny diamonds circled the larger one then trailed on either side. Her mouth dropped open. She yanked her focus from the ring to his eyes. Dancing. They were definitely dancing.

"Will you marry me?"

"Yes!"

She threw her arms around him, and the joy in his eyes equaled the kiss that came a second later. She clung to him. The adrenaline from the skydive met the high from his mouth on hers and surged through her.

A moment later clapping and whooping pulled her away. Rose petals showered over them. Streamers waved. Ryann, China and Jake, Lynn and Rich, and a few others stood around them, the girls jumping and throwing flowers. Kati stared.

"Whoop! Whoop!" Ryann yelled.

Kati laughed and looked at Reece. "When did you…"

He pulled her back into his arms. "Romantic enough for you, Miss Warrior?"

"Yes, Mr. Jernigan, even if you had to scare me half to death to do it."

His amused eyes disappeared as he lowered his head again, his mouth covering hers, scattering the last of her breathless fear and cementing the love that enlarged her heart.

Author's Note

While writing this book, God told me to be courageous. Not out loud, but through a couple of devotionals, one posted on Facebook. Be strong and of a good courage. Not everyone will agree with my portrayal of spiritual warfare. Some would have loved me to go deeper. Some would want to see actual angels and demons fighting a la Frank Peretti. But he already did a great job of that in *This Present Darkness*. I highly recommend that book if you have never read it. Some readers will think I've gone too far, talked too much about God, the Bible, and prayer, who we are in Christ, and what we can pray for. May I say to them that I still believe we use way less of God's power in us than we will ever realize. I believe in Jesus and what he did on earth. I believe in what the book of Acts shows us about who the Church is (us) and what we can do if we walk with God. We are so caught up in the world these days that we don't know what we're missing in Christ or the power that we could walk in.

I also want to say that some readers might feel guilty after reading *Warrior*. You might feel you need to be doing something like what they are doing in the book, but as I had Joshua and Reece point out, not all are called to all ministries. Each person and ministry is different. Don't feel guilty; be encouraged. If you seek God, he will answer you. If you're not involved in a ministry already, ask him what he wants you to do. It may be to visit your neighbors. It may be a prayer walk around your neighborhood. It may be to the homeless in your city. Only God can tell you. Serving God is wonderful and fulfilling and sometimes hard, but there is nothing better while we're on earth. Go for it!

Playlist

While writing my books, I love to listen to praise and worship music. Especially at the beginning, God seems to use the songs to point me in the direction he wants me to go. The characters in the book, as well as the plot, begin to get fleshed out as I listen. He puts certain songs on my heart that I listen to again and again. In this book that was even more real to me than ever.

A number of songs represented each of the main characters in the book.

For Kati, it was "All In," by Matthew West; "Break Every Chain," by Jesus Culture; and "Dry Bones (Come Alive)," sung by Lauren Daigle.

For Joshua, it was "All In," too, and "I Wanna Be Different (Different)," by Micah Tyler.

For Reece, it was "Control," by Tenth Avenue North; "If I Tell You My Story," by Big Daddy Weave; and "Greater" and "Even If," by MercyMe.

The complete list for the book (in no particular order) was:
"Control," by Tenth Avenue North
"Even If," by MercyMe
"All In," by Matthew West
"I Wanna Be Different (Different)," by Micah Tyler
"Even So Come," by Kristen Stanfill
"Break Every Chain," by Jesus Culture
"In Christ Alone," sung by Kristen Stanfill, written by Travis Cottrel
"Need You Now," by Plumb

"At the Cross," by Hillsong Worship
"If I Told You My Story," by Big Daddy Weave
"The Cross Has Made You Flawless," by MercyMe
"Good, Good Father," by Chris Tomlin
"It Is Well," by Kristine DeMarco and Bethel Music
"What a Beautiful Name," by Hillsong Worship
"Come Alive (Dry Bones)," Lauren Daigle
"Greater," by MercyMe
"No Longer Slaves," sung by Jonathan David and Melissa Helser
"Faultless," by MercyMe.
"Rooftops by Jesus Culture
"Do It Again," by Elevation Worship
"Oh Come to the Altar," by Elevation Worship

Thank You!

I want to give a special thank you for all that have prayed for this book. I knew doing one on spiritual warfare would up the need for prayer. And it did! All the prayers, however big or small, were so essential to bringing this about.

I also want to thank the beta readers whose help improved and enhanced the story. I need to mention especially Kathy Blackwell, Amarylis (Marggie) Rassler, and Linda Sollecchio. God used each of you to help bring the book to the next level.

I appreciate Lynnette Bonner so much for creating the cover and taking my request for a three-person design and making it a reality. Not an easy accomplishment, but accomplish it she did! Lynnette, thank you for putting up with me and all my questions and changes!

Dori Harrell, my editor, was again a blessing in catching all the errors I thought I already had caught! You have a great eye—and patience with my need for last-minute changes.

Thank you to others, too, like author Randy Travis, MEEZ Carrie of *Reading is My Superpower*, and interviewer Rebecca Lynn Van Daniker, who all agreed to do an interview or review before I had finished the book. You are God's encouragers!

The medical information about infection and hospital routine would not have been possible without the excellent input of Stacy Smith, RN, from Oldsmar, Florida. Thank you, Stacy, for your patience with this layman and jumping on the bandwagon when I needed someone. God bless you.

And thank you to many faithful reviewers who have been with me from the beginning, or close to it. I appreciate each one of you! Your encouragement over the years has been a great blessing!

Thank you to my husband, Frank, who has put up with me being huddled in my office again for long hours while working on this manuscript.

I could never do any of this without the Lord Jesus Christ, the Father, and the Holy Spirit. I recognize that I do not have it in me to stay the course in something like this—and it is God who encourages and pushes me on and takes the story where he wants it to go. Jesus was a storyteller (using parables), and he allows me, in a small way, to take part in that.

A Request

I hope you have enjoyed and were blessed by *Warrior*. If so, perhaps you would leave a review on Amazon and/or Goodreads? Readers and authors need and love reviews. To review this book, just click here: https://amzn.to/2Cb5nZG. Scroll down to this book, click on the reviews already there, and it will give you a place to add your review.

***

Linda's Books, in order:
Amber Alert, Book 1 of The Dangerous Series
As Long As You Both Shall Live, Book 2
Splashdown, Book 3
Looking for Justice, Book 4
Honor Respect Devotion, Book 5
Pursued, Book 6
Warrior, Book 7

Although the series is great read in order, each story is a stand-alone book, too. All Linda's books can be found on Amazon, https://amzn.to/2PW2Hln.

***

If you enjoyed this book please join Christian Indie Author Readers Group on Facebook. You will find Christian books in multiple genres and opportunities to find other Christian authors and learn about new releases, sales, and free books. https://www.facebook.com/groups/291215317668431/.

Author Biography

Linda K. Rodante is an author and lover of sweet tea now living in the foothills of Tennessee, a Florida transplant who loves the seasonal changes in Tennessee. She's married with two sons and three grandchildren.

Linda writes Christian romantic suspense. Her books wrap sweet romance in real-life issues women face today, then adds an edge of mystery and suspense. She desires not only to entertain with a good story but to encourage others in their walk with God.

Her work with crisis pregnancy centers and anti-trafficking groups have given her a heart for women struggling in today's society, while still respecting the role and strength God has given to men.

She's a member of the American Christian Fiction Writers (ACFW), of Word Weavers International, and of the Southeastern Writer's Alliance. She belongs to Christian Indie Authors, Clean Indie Reads, and many other online readers' groups, and has her own Facebook group, Christian Romantic Suspense Readers. She's a past finalist of ACFW's Genesis contests.

.

If you enjoyed *Warrior*, you might want to try the first book in the series, *Amber Alert*.

After an abusive relationship, Social worker Sharee Jones is determined to leave men alone. She'll concentrate instead on the upcoming Christmas program she's written and designed. But she'll need the church's pilot-turned-multi-skilled maintenance technician's help to do it.

John Jergenson doesn't want anything to do with Sharee's program. After a tragedy in his own life, he's angry with God and life in particular. But Sharee's enthusiasm, her warmth, her persistent getting-in-his-face attitude might have him changing his mind. Then a baby is kidnapped and Sharee decides to play detective. The ante in life just went up, and John's about to make a move he never saw coming...

https://www.amazon.com/gp/product/B0165WGPY Q/ref=dbs_a_def_rwt_bibl_vppi_i1

Here's a sneak peek of the first few pages:

Amber Alert

How many people does it take to find a baby?

Sharee Jones sent up the desperate plea to God, even as her body protested the long, wet search. Exhaustion and discouragement, enhanced by the cold December night, increased as darkness turned toward morning. Her flashlight illuminated muddy ground, and she leaned a shaking hand against a tree. Those on either side of her stopped. Sounds from other searchers echoed through the darkness. Their lights, whispered voices, and the moonlight imparted an unreal feeling to the area.

How many people does it take to find a baby? A small regiment. Or at least it seemed that way. Now that the Amber Alert had gone out, the police, the dog handlers, church members, even neighbors and strangers had joined the frantic battle against time.

Her best friend's child had vanished, and it was Sharee's fault. She'd planned the program; she'd agreed to Joshua's part in it—an infant playing baby Jesus—and since the mother and father volunteered for Mary's and Joseph's parts, well… How much better could it get?

Sharee raised her arm into a narrow wash of light. Her watch glinted. Eight hours since the baby's disappearance. The chances of finding him, and finding him alive, faded with each passing hour.

Now and again, she glanced back. The Christmas lights from the enormous six-pointed star pierced the darkness and mocked her. Peace on earth, goodwill to men? Could there be

198

any peace until they found Joshua? Sharee closed her eyes, her chest heavy and aching. The image of that first mutilated doll burst across her mind, and her eyes flew open.

Kidnapped...or worse.

She slipped on the muddy ground, and a man's hand reached out to steady her. His other caught a wet branch as it snapped back at them. Cold rain splattered their faces. Sharee pulled free, wiped the rain from her eyes, and looked at John Jergenson. He rubbed a hand across his face, too, and caught her look. She ducked her head and turned away.

No time for that, no time to think of the other disaster within the last twenty-four hours.

"Ted, we're right behind you." John's voice didn't have the exhausted quality Sharee knew hers carried now, but stress echoed in his words. "Watch the flying branches, will you?"

"Sorry." Ted Hogan's answer drifted back from the darkness ahead.

Sharee stared at the place from which Ted's voice materialized. Her beam held both pines and underbrush in an unearthly glow. Vines twisted upward, catching on anything in their way. She thanked God that Ted had joined them a short while ago. They needed all the help they could get. She, John, and Lynn Stapleton had headed out as soon as the deputy gave permission.

Earlier, the sheriff's deputies had searched the church buildings and the grounds and found nothing. This undeveloped land next door to the church had acquired major importance. Other groups were wading through the trees and brush, while some inspected the nearby pond and the stand of cypress. Officers canvassed the neighborhood.

A gasp from behind caught her attention. She glanced over her shoulder. Lynn's long blonde hair hung soaked and dripping, except for one strand caught in a long-fingered branch. Her gunmetal quilted parka glistened with moisture, and mud covered the stylish high-heeled boots. Lynn yanked the hair free.

"You okay?" Sharee shoved a hand through her own wet hair. Her jeans and sweatshirt offered no better protection than her friend's clothing.

"I'm okay. I just wish I had something to pull this back with." Lynn wrapped the waist-length hair around the top of her head once more. "If I had a clip—" She stopped and her eyes widened.

Sharee jerked around, shooting her beam across the dark foliage in front of her. Lights and faces floated, ghostlike, among the trees before emerging into features and visages she recognized.

"We're going in for a while," Pastor Alan Nichols said, stepping from the darkness. "Come with us."

Ted appeared from the gloom behind them. "Go in? No way. We can't stop."

"We're not stopping, just taking a break. It's been a long night." The pastor nodded to two soaked individuals passing them.

"Go ahead if you want." Ted's voice hardened. "But I'm staying. Lisa doesn't need us quitting."

"We're not quitting." The pastor moved aside as a third person went by him. "Daybreak's an hour away. They'll be forming a line of searchers then, covering the same ground we've covered tonight." His focus shifted to Sharee and Lynn. "In the meantime, we need to dry off and get something warm into our stomachs."

Sharee straightened and picked up her chin, but the pastor frowned before he turned to follow the others. John's light played over her, then swept past to rake Lynn in its brightness. Lynn pushed away from the tree she'd leaned against, but her boots slipped, and she grabbed for it again.

"Alan's right," he said. "We're all tired. Let's take a break. Ted, help Lynn. Those boots she's wearing weren't made for this mud."

"I'm fine," Lynn sputtered, but her teeth chattered.

"And I said I'm staying." Ted's voice grated.

"You can't stay." Sharee grimaced at the sound of her own voice, swallowed, and started again. "You can't stay. The deputy wanted us to stay in groups of three or four."

"I don't care what he wanted."

"Yeah, well, they don't want anyone out here alone. You don't want to go through another interrogation, do you?"

Ted muttered under his breath, but a moment later, he caught Lynn's arm. Sharee's heart gave a strange blip as she slipped past John's outstretched hand and headed back.

Too much tonight, Lord. It's too much.

When they reached the open field forming the church's boundary, she and Lynn dropped onto the closest bleachers. Other search groups sat together, too, speaking in whispers. Some had cups of warm liquid in their hands. Steam rose like small apparitions from them. White lights from the enormous star that stretched parallel to the ground and eight feet above it added another eerie glow to the night.

Where was Joshua? Sharee stared past the lights into the night shadows. Who had taken him and why?

Silence filled her heart. Joshua had disappeared, and it was her fault. She shoved wet curls from her face. Her body shook.

John stepped next to where she sat on the bleachers. She could feel his scrutiny but avoided his eyes. He lowered himself beside her, and his fingers feather-touched her hair. She swallowed, resisting the urge to turn to him, to bury her face against his shoulder.

After a moment, he straightened, and she followed his gaze to the end of the bleachers. Deputy Richards stood there, feet spread and arms crossed. His glance flickered past each huddled group until it reached Sharee. He looked from her to John and back again, and in the light from the Christmas star, she saw his eyes narrow.

33862950R00121

Made in the USA
Columbia, SC
11 November 2018